"A Song for My Warrior"
By
Justus Roux

Also by Justus Roux

Master Series:
My Master
Master's Ecstasy
Obey!
Sweet Rapture
Mistress Angelique
Wrath's Lust
Breathless (Has novella: Master Drake)
Love Thy Master
Dante and Angelique

The Demon Hunter Series:
Keeper of My Soul
Heavenly Surrender
Breathless (Has novella: Forever, Demon Hunter Ryo's story)
Ayden's Awakening

Barbarians of Malka Series:
Protector of My Heart
A Warrior's Will
A Song for My Warrior

Single Title
Paradise

Anthologies edited by Justus Roux:
Erotic Tales
Erotic Fantasy: Tales of the Paranormal
Who's Your Daddy?
Bosslady

Justus Roux's website www.justusroux.com

This book is a work of fiction and is meant for entertainment purposes only.

Please remember to always practice safe sex

ISBN 0-9777788-3-5

.

Chapter One

Nina looked around the Rundal spaceship. Demos and two other warriors were heading back to Earth to gather more Earth women to be mates for the warriors. Demos insisted Nina accompanied him. Niro allowed this—after all she was Demos' mate. Nina remembered this ship. It was the one that brought her to Malka...to Demos. This last year has been the happiest year of her life. She was named the first woman warrior of Malka, but more importantly she was joined with Demos.

"What is wrong?" Demos asked as he walked up to her.

"Oh nothing, I was just thinking how lucky I am." She wrapped her arms around him and held him tightly for a moment.

"You keep pressing that beautiful body of yours against me like that and I will have to take you right here."

"Mmm, that sounds pretty darn good to me."

"Demos," Ezra interrupted. "The Rundal captain said we must strap ourselves in we will be landing soon."

"Very well." He reached down and grabbed Nina's hand. "We will continue this later." He smiled down at her

He led her to a room which was right behind the cockpit.

"Leo." Demos nodded his head at the huge warrior who was already strapping himself to the seat. Leo was a massive man standing at least six foot ten inches tall; he won the Trials this year and earned the right to choose an Earth woman as a mate. Ezra who was just as big as Demos both stood six foot five, earned the right to choose an Earth woman by his unwavering loyalty to Alistair, one of the few warriors who did follow Alistair out of respect and not just out of loyalty to Niro. Niro had asked Demos to go along with the other two to pick a mate for Alistair. Alistair was busy trying to unite the tribes of the Larmat clan and didn't know that Niro was sending Demos to retrieve a female for him.

Demos made sure Nina was strapped in tight before he strapped himself in.

"How do you pick females?" Nina asked.

"A matter of chance I guess. Wherever the Rundals land the ship. We can't afford to be spotted by too many Earthlings," Demos said. "This is my first time to your home planet, I am most eager to see it."

"Malka is much more beautiful in my opinion," Nina said.

"Still, I am still anxious to see your former planet." Demos smiled at her.

"Demos, may I ask you something?"

"My flower you can ask me anything."

"What's the deal about Alistair? Everyone seems so hush-hush about him. I asked Robin why when Alistair's name is mentioned the vibe in the room gets all tensed. All Robin ever replies is that she won't spread idle gossip." Nina could sense an immediate tension fill the air.

"What do you mean? Niro chose him to unite the Larmat clans, to help them become one with the Dascon clans."

"I know that much, but…"

"Alistair is a half-breed," Leo interjected.

"Do not call him that," Ezra growled.

"Put on your ear coverings now," Demos rumbled at the two. He waited until they secured the headphones over their ears. "We don't have long before we have to put our ear coverings on too, Nina, so I will briefly explain. Alistair is a half-breed."

"What does that mean?"

"He is part Dascon from his mother and part Larmat from his father. This is rare on Malka. Most half-breeds are killed before they reach maturity, but Hakan took Alistair and his mother in and allowed them to live in the leader hut. I never asked him why he did this. I don't know, perhaps because I never saw Alistair as a half-breed I never thought to ask. Alistair is a good warrior and he is loyal to Niro that is all that matters to me."

"He doesn't look that different from any other Dascon warrior. Niro made Alistair the leader of the Larmat people while they get reorganize. If a half-breed is so bad…"

"Niro trusts Alistair. I believe that Niro also saw the fact that Alistair is part Larmat that he may understand the Larmat ways better than a pure Dascon warrior would."

"But he was raised as a Dascon warrior."

"Alistair's mother might have corrupted him out of her love for his father."

"Corrupted him?"

"Told him the ways of the Larmat people."

"That doesn't sound like corrupting to me, it sound likes she wanted him to know his father. Poor Alistair…" Nina looked up at Demos when he squeezed her hand.

"I don't see him as a half-breed and I am pleased to see that you will not either." He kissed her hand then handed her a pair of headphones. "Put this on, this will keep your ears from popping while we land."

Nina placed the headphones on. Moments later the ship started to descend. She was going to help Demos find the perfect mate for Alistair. Her stomach lurched as the ship dove down faster. She smiled when Demos grabbed her hand and held it tightly.

"Woohoo!" she cried out, causing Demos to start laughing.

ഇന്ദ്രൈ

Anne pushed the stack of papers off the table. She was getting nowhere with her investigation. A year…a whole year had past since her parents were murdered. The police were getting nowhere so she decided to start investigating on her own. She put off going to her fourth year of college. Her training to be a vet could wait. She had to find her parents' killer or killers. Her parents were murdered for loving each other. The evidence at the scene of the crime suggested it was a hate crime. The racial slurs painted on her parent's bodies…she couldn't think about it. She had to focus. Someone had to know something. She wouldn't let whoever did this get away with taking her parents from her.

She glanced at the calendar. Today would have been her parent's twenty-fifth wedding anniversary. Her parents had gone out last year to celebrate their anniversary and on their way home some one ran them off the road and brutally killed them. The killers had to have been stalking them, waiting for the right time to strike. She remembered the phone calls, an angry voice calling her an abomination, calling her parents evil for producing such a child. The police did try to trace back the calls, but the caller never stayed on long enough to get anything. Anne stood up and walked around the kitchen trying to get the memories of that angry voice out of her mind.

"It doesn't matter what narrow-minded people think. All that matters is the love that is in this house." Her father's words would always soothe her.

Her whole life she has dealt with not really belonging. Her father's family rarely saw her and when they did they always acted strange. Her mother's family had disowned her mother for marrying a white man, so

Anne never got a chance to know them. But her parents had enough love that it didn't really matter. Just seeing them together, watching them ignore the stares from strangers as they walked hand in hand together. The way her mother looked so happy just being with her father. The way they made her feel so loved.

Anne glanced around the large house. This house was once her sanctuary from the cruelties of the outside world and now it was just a reminder on how cruel the world can be.

Anne jerked hearing a strange loud noise coming from the backyard. Her heart started pounding in her chest. Somebody was definitely out there. There were no real weapons in the house—she had a problem with guns. She did have a stun gun and some pepper spray, but both were up in her bedroom. "Shit," she whispered. Anne grabbed the broom that was propped up against the counter.

"You can't just burst in there?"

Anne was puzzled hearing a woman's voice. The deep male voice that tried to hush the woman up caused Anne to grip the broom handle harder. She jumped back when the door burst opened.

"Demos, you can't do that!" Nina hurried inside behind him. Her eyes locked with the frightened woman clutching the broomstick. "Look, you have scared her." Nina slowly walked over to Anne. "We are not going to hurt you."

"Who are you people?"

"I doubt you would believe me if I told you."

"Try me."

"Come female, we must head back to the Rundal ship," Demos' voice boomed.

"Demos let me handle this."

"Rundal ship?"

"Do you have a boyfriend, husband…?"

"No…who are you?"

"I am Nina and this is my…husband Demos."

"Husband?" Demos looked at her puzzled.

"It's what a mate is called here."

"Get out of my house. You two must be crazy. I am going to call the cops." Anne dropped the broom and ran toward the phone. Before she reached it she felt herself being lifted into the air and then thrown over Demos' shoulder.

"Demos!" Nina scolded him.

"Put me down." Anne realized that Demos was only wearing a loincloth and that there was a very large sword strapped to his back. She looked to Nina and saw she wore some kind of fur top and a strange shimmering fabric for pants, and that she too had a sword strapped to her back.

"Don't struggle female. We have no wish to harm you." Demos tried to keep his voice gentle.

"I am sorry, but trust me where you are going is much better."

"Where am I going?" Anne started to pound on Demos' back. "Let me go asshole."

"We have to get her on the ship," Demos said, heading for the door. He had to hold Anne tightly to his shoulder as she struggled violently to free herself.

Nina looked down at all the papers tossed around the kitchen floor. She went to pick one of the papers up…

"Don't touch those," Anne shouted as she struggled harder to free herself. Demos' grip was like iron and all she was managing to do was to wear herself out.

"Demos…this feels strange. I remembered when I was just taken like this." Nina watched the violent way Anne fought. Hell she was just like that when Rai captured her a year ago.

"You said this female would be perfect for Alistair. Now we must go."

"You looked so sad when I saw you through the window, may I ask why?" Nina asked Anne.

"No…now let me down."

Demos headed out the door and straight for a beam of light.

"Demos!" Nina hurried to him.

"We must go my flower." Demos looked down at Nina. He could see the guilt creeping into her eyes. "I have taken this woman aboard you haven't done anything." With that Demos stepped into the beam.

Anne felt funny and it took her eyes a moment to adjust. This big man still had her over his shoulder and was carrying her somewhere. She couldn't make out where she was. She looked behind them and saw the woman from earlier.

"I am sorry," Nina said. It felt wrong to just take this woman. But Demos' people would die out if they didn't. So far Robin and Sabrina had children, and Jamie was with child. Nina however hasn't gotten pregnant yet. The Malka infants were rather large and as such it is feared that the Earth women would only produce one offspring. Tomar, the leader of the Rundal, was monitoring all the Earth women carefully. Until Niro was sure that no harm was going to come to the Earth women only a couple at a time was brought to Malka. Tomar had scouts searching other planets as well, looking for compatible females for the Malka males.

Demos carefully set Anne down and left the room. He closed and locked the door then looked down at Nina. That look on her face bothered him.

"I didn't like being dragged from my home," Nina said. She slowly looked up at Demos. "But if I hadn't been I would have never met you."

"Alistair will make her very happy." Demos took Nina into his arms. "When the female has settled down, you should go talk to her."

"Don't call her female. I hated that part too."

"When I learn her name then I won't call her female. Nina, why did you pick this female?"

"She looked so sad. I figured she might stand a chance of being happy on Malka."

"I don't think Ezra and Leo chose their females with such care as you did."

"Yeah, speaking of them where are they?"

"With their females."

"Oh no…Demos we can't let them try and rape those two women."

"Who says they are going to take them against their will?"

"I just remember spending the whole trip to Malka fighting off Rai."

"Ezra and Leo are not like Rai was. They are like me in regards to females. But if it makes you feel better I will request that they allow you to talk to their females."

"That would be great. Those poor women are probably frightened."

"Demos, we must prepare to launch," the Rundal captain announced.

"Then I guess we better head back to our chamber." Demos smiled such a wickedly sexy smile at Nina.

"Mmm, sounds good to me." Nina grabbed his hand and led him back to their chamber.

৯০৯০৯০

Anne pounded on the steel door. "Let me out of here, damn it." She pounded and pounded until her hands were sore. She felt a strange tickling sensation in her belly and her body became slightly off balance. She grabbed the rail of the bedpost and held on to balance herself. The ship must be taking off.

"No, no damn it no!" she screamed as she tried to pull herself back to the door. "You can't do this to me. I can't leave, you can't take me." Her voice began to shake as she realized the hopelessness of her situation. She sank down to her knees still holding the bedrail. After a few moments her balance returned. She remained there on her knees.

She stayed like that for an hour. When her strength returned she stood up and headed back to the door. She began pounding on the door again. She jumped back when the door slid open. She slowly stepped back away from Demos.

"What is wrong?" he asked. Her pounding against the door and her screaming was echoing through the ship.

"What is wrong? What the fuck do you think is wrong? Take me back...take me back now."

"I am afraid I can't do that."

Anne stepped back further when Demos walked into the room, he closed the door behind him. "My mate will be here soon. She will try to calm you down."

"Fuck her and fuck you." Anne grabbed the nearest thing next to her and threw it at Demos. He ducked to avoid being hit in the head by the stone vase. Anne grabbed plates and glasses, vases and books—she whipped each one at Demos. He avoided all of them.

"You better calm down," his voice more stern.

"The hell I will. Take me back to my house now!" She grabbed a large piece of stone art and using all her strength threw it at him. He stepped out of the way.

She gasped when he charged at her.

"Don't touch me...don't fucking touch me." She hit him over and over until he pinned her hands behind her back.

"I will not hurt you, but you need to stop acting like a spoil child."

"Spoil child..." She kicked him in his leg as hard as she could, but it didn't seem to faze him at all.

"Calm down, female."

"My name is Anne, not female."

"Demos what in the hell are you doing to her?" Nina asked as she entered the room. She became instantly jealous seeing Demos holding that woman so close to him.

"Trying to restrain her."

Nina looked around at all the items that were strewn across the room.

"Tell your husband to let me go."

"Demos let her go. I don't think she has anything left to throw at you."

Demos slowly let her go and stepped back. He glanced over to Nina and saw slight anger in her eyes. "What is wrong, my flower?"

"I walk in here and you are holding some strange female...I am going to be just a little ticked off."

"But..."

"You couldn't find a better way to calm her down."

"I..."

"How would you like it if I held another warrior like that?"

"I would kill him."

Anne watched the couple arguing. "I don't want your husband. I want you to take me back home."

"Quiet female," Demos growled, causing Anne to step back further.

"Demos...you can't yell at her she is already traumatized enough."

"I don't like it when you are angry with me. I meant no disrespect to you by restraining this female. You are the only female who will have use of my body."

"I know that, you big lug. I just didn't like seeing you holding another female. I got jealous."

"Nina…you forgive me?"

"Of course I do. But I would think it would be best if you let me talk with her for a little while."

Demos grabbed Nina and pulled her to him. He kissed her deeply holding her very close.

"Oh geez, do you flippin mind?" Anne looked away from the couple. She heard Demos' heavy footsteps leave the room.

"What's your name?"

"It's Anne."

"I am Nina."

"I want you to take me back to my home."

"I can't do that."

"One way or another I am going to go back home." Anne grabbed the perfume bottles on the vanity and started throwing them at Nina.

Nina hurried from the room. She locked the door then leaned against it.

"She will be most difficult," Demos said.

"That is an understatement."

Chapter Two

Alistair sat in his chamber. This last year was tough. Trying to keep the Dascon males from taking the Larmat females had proved to be difficult. The Larmat males would often fight with the Dascon males, not to protect the females but more as a matter of pride. Alistair didn't understand the Larmat way of thinking. A female was only property to these males and this mentality was rubbing off on some of the Dascon males. He wanted to just send half of his warriors home, but Niro wouldn't allow it, especially now with the rumors of a Larmat uprising brewing.

Alistair was eager to learn more about his father's clan. However, the more he learned the more he didn't understand his mother's love of such a man. These Larmat people seemed so much more barbaric than the Dascon people. Less interested in what was good for all of Malka and more interested in what they could acquire. Was his father just like the majority of them, or was he somehow different? Is that what earned his mother's love? These questions would have to wait. Now Alistair had to focus on bringing order to these lands. Niro entrusted him with the task and he wasn't about to let him down. Niro was one of the handful of warriors who didn't see Alistair as a half-breed and for this he was grateful. When Hakan died Alistair mourned him. He could never repay Hakan for his kindness to him and his mother. Alistair could still hear the grumbling voices of warriors wanting to kill him and punish his mother. Hakan's loud voice silenced them all and forbade anyone to harm them. Years later when Alistair asked Hakan why he spared him and his mother all Hakan replied, "*It was wrong to punish a female for loving her male. Besides Alistair I knew you would make a fine warrior. You symbolize what it should be, Larmat and Dascon living in peace.*" From that moment on, Alistair swore his undying loyalty to Hakan and now to Hakan's son Niro. Niro had the same vision for Malka...peace.

Alistair looked up when he heard his chamber door open. A smaller Larmat female entered the room. Her long, golden blonde hair ran the length of her back, her face was sweet almost innocent looking. This female had just reached maturity.

"Great leader," she whispered as she slowly approached him. She came down to her knees before him. "I am from the village Exoida. I offer myself as tribute."

"Tribute?" Alistair stood up and looked down at the kneeling woman. He watched as she began to remove her clothes. "Stop." He reached down and helped her to her feet. "You need not come to your knees before me or give your body to me."

"But great leader, my village sent me as tribute. I know Dascon blood also runs in your veins, but I am prepared to offer my body for your use."

"Dascon blood..."

"Your Larmat blood is tainted with the Dascon blood."

"Half-breed, just come out and say it," his voice boomed, causing her to back away from him. "Go back to your village, female. I will not have you sacrifice your virtue to bed a half-breed."

"Great leader...I didn't mean to anger you." She rushed to him and fell to her knees, she grabbed his leg. "I can't go back, if you refuse me I will be an outcast in my village."

"Then you will know my plight."

"Please forgive my words…I didn't mean to insult you, great leader." She started moving her hands up his leg. "It would be an honor to bring you pleasure."

Alistair stopped her hand before she reached his cock. It had been so long since he had been with a female. When the people saw him as the Larmat leader each village sent their most beautiful female to belong to him. And each one of these females were just like this one, only doing their duty, they had no desire to be with a half-breed. He could see it in their eyes or they were as bold as this one is and just tell him. No, he didn't want to take a female who didn't want him, even if his body ached to know the pleasures of a female. He had only been with one female before after he was named one of the Grand warriors. But she too seemed repulsed to be with a half-breed. Larmat or Dascon none of their females wanted to give themselves willing to him.

"I will not send you back, but I will not use your body either." Alistair pulled her up to her feet. He walked her over to the door and motioned for the guard to come over. "Take her to the female quarters. Don't touch her." Alistair glared at the large warrior. The woman quietly followed the Dascon warrior. Alistair could only hope that the warrior would obey his command and not touch the female.

There were no weaker males anywhere in the Larmat villages. They simply killed the males that weren't strong enough to be warriors. They didn't use them as outlets for their lust like the Dascon warriors did. With no weaker males, Alistair was finding it hard to stop the Dascon warriors that were here with him from taking the females.

The Larmat warriors did honor their elder warriors this was one thing that the two clans had in common. Any warrior proving his valor on the battlefield could enjoy his life off the battlefield once he was too old to fight anymore. These warriors had mates by then, if they survived the countless battles they were entitled to a mate. Most warriors however didn't survive the battlefields, so elder males were rare on Malka. A fact that Niro's mate Robin recently noticed.

Alistair liked Robin, she was good for Niro and she was a good mother, though her cause to improve the lives of the weaker males was not a popular thing with the Dascon warriors. Alistair admired her resolve. Niro's son Zenos was growing stronger everyday. Alistair enjoyed seeing the little guy when he visited the main village of Dascon. Though now his visits were getting further and further apart. Niro was coming here to see how well Alistair was doing and help him out a bit. He doubted that Niro would bring Robin and Zenos with him. He hoped that Niro did bring Demos and Nina with him. It would be nice to see Demos again. He liked to spar with Demos. Nina…he was impressed by her battle skills, but more impressed by her refusal to be what is expected of a female. The fact the Demos allowed Nina the freedom to do this was amazing. Demos didn't care what the other warriors thought, he never really did. He judged a person for who they were. Alistair had great respect for Demos.

Alistair looked around the lush chamber. This was the chamber where Malin and then Rasmus had lived in. Alistair had gone to battle with both of these former Larmat leaders and now he lives where they once did.

"Alistair," a large Dascon warrior said as he entered the chamber.

"What is it?" Alistair turned toward the warrior.

"Niro has sent word that he will be arriving in four days, he will have his mate and child with him, and I assume that means there will be many Dascon warriors coming with him. He also said to tell you he had a surprise for you."

"A surprise? Is Demos and his mate Nina coming with them?" Alistair tried to imagine what the surprise might be.

"Of course Demos is coming, Niro is bringing his mate with him. Alistair, if I may be so bold but to ask something?"

"Go ahead."

"Why do you not enjoy the females that are given to you?"

"I will not take a female that doesn't want me."

"Why not, she is offering her body to you; why not take pleasure from her."

"I have my reasons. Tell the servants to ready the chamber for Niro and his warriors."

"Yes Alistair."

Alistair felt his mood lighten. He looked forward to Niro's visit. Maybe Niro could help him make sense of these Larmat people. This year he had little time to explore the Larmat culture, he had visited village after village letting the people see their new leader. He wanted to ease the people's fears and assure them that he was no tyrant. Alistair wanted to understand the other half of himself, but he saw himself as a warrior for the Dascon clan. Just because Larmat blood ran in his veins didn't mean that he would understand the people. The only thing he had to go on was what his mother told him about his father. After being around these people he had even more trouble believing her stories on how his father risked everything to bring her back to her Dascon village. How he stole moments to be with her, knowing if he was caught it would mean death. He barely remembered his father's face. The only thing he remembered was his father's long golden hair. He was only four when his mother took him to live with Hakan. His mother's profound sadness when they entered the main Dascon village was the one thing that has been burnt into his memory.

Alistair walked to the door. He had to clear his head and prepare for Niro's visit. He could only hope that Niro would be pleased with the progress he had made so far bringing these villages together. What he needed now was to train until his arms and legs ached.

Chapter Three

Anne looked out across Dascon from her balcony. Nina had brought her to this chamber when they arrived at the village. Anne didn't say much to anyone. This was all too bizarre, the spaceship, these barbarians, this planet…she was having trouble absorbing it all. Nina had tried to talk with her on the ship, but Anne just wanted to be alone. Now Anne was expected to meet the leader of these barbaric people. Perhaps she should have talked with Nina and at least learned more about this planet.

She took a deep breath to calm herself. She was here now and she'd best figure out what here was. There was a strange peace to this village. She could see it, hell she could feel it.

She couldn't stop feeling anxious it was more than being swept away to this planet it was the thought of failing her parents. A year of her life dedicated to finding the people responsible for taking her parents away. Now she was stuck here on the planet of huge males wearing loincloths. It was so preposterous, this can't possibly be real. She told herself this over and over in the ship, trying to talk herself out of believing this was really happening to her. But there was no denying it anymore. She needed to find a way to reason with these people. Perhaps talking with the leader of these people wasn't so bad after all. He would have the power to send her back.

She quickly turned around when she heard the chamber door open. Her eyes locked with the gorgeous green-eyed barbarian that stood in the doorway.

"My name is Niro. I am the leader of the Dascon clan."

Niro looked at the brown-skin female. Never had he seen a female like this. He took a moment to appreciate her beauty, her full lips, dark eyes and shoulder-length dark hair. She was most beautiful and would make a very suitable match for Alistair, though to Niro no female was more beautiful than Robin.

"Nina tells me your name is Anne."

"Yes." Anne could barely speak. This man before her was the ruler of all these barbarian warriors. What if she did something to piss him off? How was she supposed to act? God she hoped he wasn't expecting her to fall to her knees, kiss his hand or whatever rulers expect of their subjects.

"You needn't fear me."

"How do I address you?"

"Address me?"

"What am I suppose to call you?"

"Niro." Niro moved closer to her. Nina explained to him this female's reluctance to talk with anyone. Maybe Robin could get through to Anne. "I would like you to come with me." He turned and started walking out of the chamber. He looked back and was pleased that Anne was following him. Robin would have to explain to Anne about Malka. He didn't want to bring Anne to Alistair before she understood what was going on. The other two Earth women were adapting well. He was glad he allowed Nina to go with Demos to Earth, this seemed to help the females adjust quicker. He would have to keep this in mind for future trips to Earth.

Anne could hear a child crying as they approached the two large doors. The closer they got she heard a woman gently singing to the child. This brought her comfort. All forms of music eased her mind. She watched Niro slowly opening one of the large doors. He was trying so hard not to make any noise. This made Anne smile. She stood beside Niro when they entered the chamber.

"The female is my mate Robin and she holds my son Zenos," Niro whispered to Anne.

Anne looked at the petite woman with long dark hair gently cradling the child as she sung a song Anne didn't recognize. Judging by the size of the child he had to be at least two years old. She looked up at Niro he had such a warm smile on his face watching Robin.

"You're once, twice, three times a lady…and I love you…" Anne could hear her father's voice in her mind. He loved to sing this song to her mother. The gentle way he held her in his arms as he serenaded her. The way he would kiss her hand then rush over to Anne when she was little and scooped her up in his arms and sing a little to her too.

Niro looked down at Anne when she started to cry.

"It's alright." Niro placed his arm around her and was surprised when she latched onto him. She didn't care that she barely knew this man. The flood of memories that washed over wouldn't stop. Niro looked over to Robin. He didn't know what to do. He knew how to comfort Robin, but he was unsure how to bring comfort to this female.

Robin placed Zenos in his playpen and hurried over to Niro.

"What is wrong?" Robin grabbed Anne's hand. She offered Anne the comfort of her arms. Anne released Niro and slowly allowed Robin to hold her.

"Your singing just reminded me…" Anne held Robin tighter.

"Reminded you of what?"

"I would rather not say."

"That's alright. Come on let's sit down and get to know each other."

Zenos started to cry again. Niro went over to him and picked him up. Zenos quieted down right away.

"He wanted his father," Robin said.

"Your son is very cute. How old is he?" Anne quickly pulled herself together. She felt like a fool breaking down in front of these strangers like that.

"He is a year old."

"One year old, he is a big boy I thought he looked more like a two year old."

"Well, his daddy is a big man. Malka children are much bigger than Earth children."

"I am going to take my son to the training grounds. Anne you stay and talk with Robin." Niro started walking to the door.

"Whoa wait a minute, you are not taking our son to the training grounds he is liable to get hurt."

"Nina will be there. I want my son to see his father train. I promise he will be just fine."

"Niro, Zenos is only a year old. He won't understand what he is watching."

"Niro, Robin is right. Zenos is much too young to watch his father train. He will only think you are hurting the other warriors," Kelila said as she entered the chamber. She took Zenos from Niro.

"Next year Zenos will start his training." Niro went over to Robin and kissed her sweetly then he left the chamber.

"I remember when Hakan wanted to take Niro out on the training grounds this young. Niro is so much like his father." Kelila smiled over at Anne.

"This is Anne," Robin said. "Anne this is Niro's mother Kelila."

"Alistair's female?" Kelila asked

"Yes."

"What does that mean?" Anne looked at both women.

"You are very beautiful," Kelila commented as she sat down next to Anne.

"Thank you, but what does Alistair's female suppose to mean."

"Robin will explain everything to you. Your skin has such a nice complexion are there more females like you on Earth?"

"Kelila, Earth women come in a wide range of complexions," Robin said.

"Really, this is most interesting."

"Whoa wait." Anne stood up; she tried to keep her voice calm as not to upset Zenos. "What does Alistair's female mean?"

"You were chosen to become Alistair's mate," Robin said.

"Alistair is a grand warrior and is the acting ruler of the Larmat clan," Kelila added.

"Mate? As in wife?"

"Yes."

"Hey, I don't even know this Alistair and for that matter I didn't ask to be brought to this...planet...and I want to know what in the hell is going on!"

"Please calm down. Kelila could you take Zenos to your chamber?"

"My pleasure."

Robin waited for Kelila to leave. "I am sorry you were taken from Earth. I was too a few years ago. Niro wishes there was another way, but his people are endangered of becoming wiped out. A strange illness killed most of the women on this planet and that stupid war killed many more. The Rundals, which you will be meeting their leader Tomar shortly, are the ones that found Earth and discovered that the women might be able to mate with Malka males. As you can see, Zenos is very healthy so it is proof that this is so. The only problem is that the Malka infants are so large that Tomar fears I will only be able to give Niro one child. This will not help Niro's people."

"These people are endangered?"

"Yes, with too few females there are not enough children being born and eventually their race will die out."

Anne sat down on the bed. "Why me? Why those other two women, why you?"

"Random chance, but I am so grateful that Niro found me. I have never been so happy. I doubt I could have lived such a life on Earth. There is so much you need to know. I wish you would have let Nina talk to you on the ship."

"I have something I have to finish on Earth." Anne hoped that Robin would listen. Robin seemed gentle and strangely she felt at ease around her.

"What is it?"

Anne sat silent for a moment. "My parents were murdered last year and their killers have still not been found. I have to find the scum that took their lives."

"Oh...I am so sorry."

"So you see I have to go back." Anne looked at Robin hopefully, silently pleading that she would be able to help her.

"The Rundal ship will be leaving in six months I will make sure that you and Alistair go with them."

"Alistair?" Anne looked at Robin puzzled.

"I am sorry, but Niro has decreed that you are Alistair's mate. And besides you can't reject Alistair."

"The hell I can't."

"Please..." Robin grabbed Anne's hand. "Alistair has known nothing but rejection his whole life."

"Why? What's wrong with him?"

"On Earth there would be more understanding for Alistair, but not here."

"What's wrong with him?"

"Alistair is what they call a half-breed."

Anne pulled her hand away from Robin and stood up. *Half-breed*, how many times had she heard those words from the lips of cruel ignorant people on Earth when they used to taunt her.

"There are two races of barbarians on Malka, the Larmat and the Dascon, Alistair comes from both which makes him an outcast here. Niro's father Hakan took Alistair and his mother in and trained Alistair to be a warrior. Niro helped make Alistair a grand warrior and he trust Alistair enough to let him rule the Larmat clans while they try to unite all the villages on Malka. Niro wanted Alistair to have a mate, to have someone to bring him comfort and in time love."

Anne just stood there. She had screamed and yelled, begged and pleaded and even resorted to violence and not one of these damn barbarians would listen to her. It was obvious they had no intention on taking her back at least this Robin gave her a little hope. What other choice did she have but to accept this woman's offer. "I will meet this Alistair, but you have to promise me two things. One, that I will not be forced to be his mate and two that I will go back to Earth in six months so I can find my parents killers."

"Alright, I couldn't force you to be Alistair's mate, he has to prove himself to you then you accept him."

"But you just said Niro wanted me to be Alistair's mate."

"If you accept Alistair…you have a lot to learn, but we must get ready to go to the main Larmat village."

"Why?"

"So you can meet Alistair."

Chapter Four

Rodan sat by the campfire with his twin brother Ivor. They and their growing number of warriors had to be careful of Alistair's warriors. They were always moving from one village to the next trying to stay one step ahead. It would look suspicious to have such a large number of warriors grouped together. Rodan was the leader of this group. He was determined not to let that half-breed Alistair rule his people. He had no desire to unite the Larmat clan with the Dascon clan, as Niro would like to see.

"Niro is on his way to the main Larmat village. I just heard that from the villagers," Ivor said as he poked at the fire.

"Then we must be careful. Rumors of our rebellion have no doubt reached Alistair by now," Rodan added.

"If only we had more warriors we could kill the Dascon leader along with that half-breed."

"Patience Ivor, we must go about this in the right way. If we attack now we will only waste good warriors. No doubt Niro will be escorted by several of those filthy Dascon warriors."

"Once we have killed Alistair our people will recognize you as their leader, Rodan."

"Yes Ivor, then the Larmat clan will be returned to the way it has always been."

"Alistair is always surrounded by his Dascon warriors. If only we could draw him out."

"You will think of something."

"I want you Ivor to travel to the main village."

"Me?"

"Alistair doesn't know who the warriors are that revolt against him. You will just be another Larmat warrior to him. I trust you above all others brother. While you gather all the information you can on Alistair I will look for more warriors to join us."

"I will leave first thing tomorrow morning."

ಕಾಕಾಕಾ

Anne held on to Nina for dear life. When Nina told her they would be flying to the main Larmat village Anne didn't envision they would be doing that on the back of a creature that look like a dragon. Nina said this creature was called a conja. Demos gave Nina this conja for their year anniversary, which she affectionately called Susie. They had been traveling for two days now. They camped to sleep for the night then they spent the rest of the day flying on these darn creatures. Anne wanted nothing more than to get off this beast.

"Look Anne the main Larmat village," Nina said.

Anne looked to the horizon and saw the large village in the distance. It was enormous just like the main Dascon village. It seemed to be simpler in design, no lavish towers like the Dascon village, but still pretty impressive. Anne grew more nervous as they got closer to the village.

"The Larmat are a bit different than the Dascon people," Nina said.

"They look different?"

"Well no, other than they have blond hair. It's just their customs are different. I am not sure how much Alistair has changed things."

"You said he was only the leader for a year, I doubt too much has changed. You can't force a race of people to change overnight."

"You are right, Anne. I doubt Niro would want the Larmat people to give up all their traditions. Now you better hold on tight we are coming in for a landing."

Anne held Nina even tighter as Susie started to descend. Anne closed her eyes tightly. She began to wonder what Alistair looked like, wondered if he was a kind or cruel man. It didn't really matter—she agreed to meet with Alistair and nothing more. In six months she was going to head home with or without him. But for now she would at least start learning about this strange world. The creatures here were fascinating; unlike anything she had seen on Earth. Maybe, this Alistair could find a way to get her home sooner. He was after all the leader of this other race of barbarians.

"You are going to like Alistair," Nina said as Susie landed.

Anne was going to be friendly with Alistair. There was no point being cruel. So far all these barbarians have been nothing but kind to her. She could at least return their kindness.

Anne could hear little Zenos giggling in the background. He enjoyed flying on the conja with Niro.

"A little baby took that trip better than me," Anne chuckled as Demos helped her off Susie.

Demos just smiled at her.

"Alistair," Nina whispered to Anne as a large, light brown-haired barbarian walked toward them.

Anne's breath caught when he came closer. He was absolutely gorgeous. His pale blue eyes were so alive with emotion. His face was chiseled and...perfectly male. His smile was perfect. His body was strong and he had to be at least six foot six. She watched as he greeted Niro then Robin and Zenos. Oh no this can't be Alistair...oh hell no. She was hoping that he would have been more barbaric looking even somewhat mean looking it would have been so much easier to keep her distance from him. She sure the hell wasn't expecting this beautiful male. His face had a gentleness about it, his eyes had such life but yet such sadness.

"I have a surprise for you," Niro said as he led Alistair over to Anne.

"Demos...Nina." Alistair greeted them. Alistair's eyes locked with Anne's.

"This is Anne and I have brought her to be your female."

Anne watched as Alistair slowly walked over closer to her. She couldn't look away. She couldn't deny or stop the way her body ignited under the heaviness of his gaze. Hell no, no....no...she couldn't be getting aroused. This wasn't how it was suppose to be.

"Anne." Alistair bowed his head slightly to her, though he was unable to take his eyes off of her. His heart pounded in his chest, his body ignited with pure raw desire.

"It's nice to meet you, Alistair," she barely got out. The way he said her name, his voice was very deep and soft...*stop it girl, just stop it.*

"Thank you, Niro." Alistair couldn't move nor stop staring at Anne's beauty.

Anne started to become uncomfortable from the intensity of his gaze. *Please someone get him away for me.* She had to think, had to come up with a new plan.

"Alistair we must get settled in. You may gaze at your female later," Niro said.

"Come, I will show you to your rooms." Alistair reluctantly turned from Anne.

Nina lightly grabbed Anne's arm. "I told you, you would like Alistair." She smiled.

"He is beautiful," she whispered. Anne started to follow Nina. She wasn't expecting to feel like this by just looking at Alistair. He awoken her desire, something she hasn't felt in quite some time. However Niro referring to her as Alistair's female was a bit annoying. She was nobody's female. She followed Nina. She looked behind her and saw Demos was right behind them. It seemed like he was never too far from Nina, for that matter Niro was never too far from Robin either. They all seemed happy, just like her parents were together. She wasn't lucky like that—she never really had that kind of love before.

The village was bustling. They walked through the market area. Anne listened as Nina explained how the people from different villages came to trade with each other. Anne noticed that all the men were large and quite frankly rather attractive. There were few women and children. But unlike the Dascon village these women didn't have protectors with them. Robin explained to her the need for a male protector, with so few women around it was dangerous to walk around alone. Yet, here the women did.

"I thought females needed protectors?" Anne asked Nina.

"Larmat women don't have protectors. They belong to males."

"Belong?"

"They don't have a say in which male takes them. Usually they try to gain favor with the strongest males hoping that he might protect her from the others."

"Well, that's a bunch of crap."

"I told you the Larmat people were different. You should never go out on your own. It's even more dangerous for a female here than it is in the Dascon village."

Anne turned to the sound of metal being hammered. A sword maker was busy doing his craft. There was such a buzz in the air as the people went about their daily lives.

"Oh, what is that?" Anne said, pointing at the pig-like creature.

"That is a Trof. Though both clans eat this animal it is a favorite with the Rundal," Nina said.

"Wasn't I supposed to meet with the Rundal leader? Quite honestly I am curious to see what lizard people look like."

"Tomar was taken back to the Rundal village on important business." Nina smiled at Anne. "I do like your curious nature. I am sure Alistair would be more than happy to show you everything."

"You are not going to leave me alone with him are you?" Anne grabbed Nina's arm. She couldn't be expected to be left alone with him.

"Of course I am. You two got to get to know each other. Besides, I saw the way you looked at him."

"I…well…all these warriors are rather attractive, a girl would have to be blind not to notice."

"Yeah, but the way you stared at Alistair…"

"Could we please change the subject?"

"Don't worry Anne, Alistair won't hurt you."

"Don't go anywhere without him," Demos added. "Or if he wishes I will guard you."

Anne looked back at Demos. He was busy scanning the area.

"Did you hear me, Anne?" He looked down at her.

"Yes."

"You must listen to Demos. It is very dangerous to walk around alone." Nina grabbed Anne's hand and led her through the small crowd.

They were greeted by two large Larmat warriors at the entrance to the leader hut. There was a strange tension to the air. Anne suspected that the Larmat warriors didn't like the fact Niro and all these Dascon warriors were here. Every one of these warriors, be it Dascon or Larmat seemed a bit on edge right now.

Inside the hut looked similar to Niro's large hut back at the Dascon village. Everything looked handmade which gave it a real charm. Anne's curious eyes took in everything. The little nuances the people of this village had set them apart from the Dascon people. This was just the surface.

They were shown to the top level of the hut, there Alistair greeted Niro. Anne kind of hid behind Demos trying to avoid eye contact with Alistair.

"These upper rooms are for your use Niro."

"Thank you Alistair. Once I have settled in Robin and Zenos I will join you in your meeting room. I am most eager to hear what you have done since the last time we spoke. Take your female and get her settled into her room and I will meet you within the hour."

"Yes Niro."

Alistair walked back toward Demos. "It is good to see you again Demos. We must spar while you are here."

"I would like that." Demos stepped aside leaving Anne standing there.

"Alistair it is always nice to see you." Nina smiled.

"As it is you, Demos' mate."

"Anne, me and Demos are going to get settled in. Alistair will show you to your room." Nina grabbed Demos hand and led him down the hall.

Anne slowly looked up when she felt the heat of Alistair's gaze.

"Please follow me."

Anne only nodded her head and then followed behind him. She was so nervous, so unsure of what to do. She continued to follow him to the lower floor of the leader hut. He led her to a large room.

"This is my chamber," he said, stepping aside once he entered.

"Yours?"

"Yes, this is where you will be staying."

"With you?"

"If you wish." Alistair felt so awkward. "If you are uncomfortable around me I will understand."

"It's just…I don't even know you." Why was he being so reasonable? She could come up with a better defensive plan if he was a pushy asshole.

Anne turned from him, she felt so strange. She about jumped out of her skin when he gently caressed her shoulder.

"You needn't fear me," he whispered. "I won't make you do anything against your will." His hand gently traced down her arm. He knew he shouldn't touch her. She seemed so afraid of him, but he couldn't stop himself. "Your skin has been kissed by the suns and yet it is so soft."

"Please allow me some time to adjust," she said, stepping away from him. Just his simple touch and his scent ignited her body further. She had to get some distance between them.

"As you wish, I will have a female bring you some food and drink."

Anne turned toward Alistair. "Thank you," she said quietly.

Alistair bowed his head then left the room.

Anne walked over to the large fur covered bed. She sat down then slowly lay down in the soft furs. Alistair's clean masculine scent filled her nostrils. She brought one of the fur blankets up to her face and nuzzled it to her cheek. This was preposterous, how could just the scent of him make her body come alive like this. She didn't want to think about it too much, not now. Somehow she had to convince this Alistair to help her get back to Earth. How was she supposed to do that? She wrapped herself in the fur and drifted off to sleep.

ೞೞೞ

"Look at her," a female voice quietly said.

"She is from Earth," another added.

"Niro's mate is from Earth too and doesn't have sun kissed skin."

"Her skin must feel like leather."

Anne could feel two hands touch her leg.

"Her skin is as soft as mine."

"What does it matter? As far as I am concern let this Earth female have that half- breed Alistair. It will spare a Larmat female from lying with him."

Anne pretended to just wake up. She startled the two women.

"Alistair has instructed us to bring you food and drink. I hope we didn't wake you."

"It is okay." Anne looked at the two blond-haired women. They were a bit smaller than the Dascon women were.

"You know…"The smaller of the two poured Anne some water. "You can refuse Alistair if you want. Niro will insist that Alistair follow the Dascon way of mating."

"What are you talking about?" Anne got up from the bed.

"A Dascon female chooses her mate. Not like us Larmat females who are just taken by the stronger warriors."

The other one set out some food. "I wouldn't blame you if you did."

"Who are you two?"

"We belong to Alistair. Since he is the acting leader of the Larmat he can have several females."

"Don't look so shocked Earth female. Alistair hasn't touched either of us. For which we are grateful."

"Please leave." Anne gestured to the door. She hated the venom these two women spewed. Low whispers and words of hate only drudged up painful memories for her.

"Oh very well." Both women left.

Anne looked over the tray of food. She didn't feel much like eating.

Anne headed for the door as she swung it opened, there was Alistair. The hateful words the two women just spoke rang in her ears as she looked up into his handsome face.

"What is wrong?"

"Would it be okay if I were to speak with Robin?"

"If this is your wish, please allow me to escort you."

"Thank you."

Alistair had such a soft, but yet deep voice. She couldn't stop herself from wondering if he always spoke with such calmness.

Alistair led her to Niro's chamber. "If you wish to go back to your chamber, let Robin get an escort for you," he said as she opened the door for her.

"Okay."

He simply nodded his head to her then left. Anne walked into the chamber and saw Robin sitting out on the balcony.

"Hello Anne, please come and join me."

Anne walked over and sat down next to Robin.

"You look upset."

"I had two women whispering in my chamber, whispering about Alistair. They called him a half-breed. I know you told me that is what he was referred to…how bad is it for him?"

"Oh I just hate it when people do that. Whispering and gossiping behind some- one's back like that. Let's put it this way as far as I know Alistair is the only half-breed who has made it to maturity. The only reason he did was because his Larmat father loved his Dascon mother and did everything to keep them safe."

"Surely there had to be other children produced between the two clans."

"No, Larmat females don't journey beyond their clan's borders and the Dascon women who were taken prisoner are only used as sex slaves. So the fact that Alistair's parents loved each other is a rarity."

"But how did they meet?"

"Alistair's mother was taken prisoner and brought to this village. Apparently Alistair's father was a grand warrior for the Larmat clan and had several Larmat females. I am not sure the particulars on the circumstances of their meeting—you would have to ask Alistair."

"So he freed her."

"He provided for them until he died then Hakan took Alistair and his mother in."

"But how?"

"Again you would have to ask Alistair."

"I know what it is like to have people whispering…"

Robin gently grabbed her hand. "But unlike Earth where not everyone is closed minded, here on Malka things are different. Niro, Demos and a few other warriors respect Alistair for the warrior he is. Most other warriors see Alistair as a freak. And yet Alistair has risen above it and proved himself first to Hakan and now to Niro. You have to admire a man like that."

"Yes you do." Anne leaned back in her chair and watched the blazing purple of the two suns setting off in the horizon. Thoughts of her father filled her mind. He was so strong and so protective of her mother and her. He always seemed to have a warm smile on his face. He shielded her from ignorant people's cruel words and when he couldn't he would always soothed her. He had fought to protect her mother that night—his body was riddled with bullet holes as he used his body to shield her mother. *I will find who did that to you daddy? I will find them and make sure they pay.* She held back her tears wanting to keep the pain she felt inside private. She felt Robin squeeze her hand tighter. Robin said nothing. Anne was grateful for that.

Chapter Five

Alistair sat in the history vault of the Larmat village with Niro. Niro was amazed by the large amount of written history the Larmat people had managed to collect. It far out shadowed the Dascon records.

"They wrote everything. They assigned the older females to the task of record keeping," Alistair said.

"Where are these females?"

"In the chambers just off of these vaults."

"Are they treated well?"

"More so than the younger females, but still their freedom is limited."

"Have you managed to read any of these?"

"Some…"

Niro turned to Alistair. "Did you find out about your father?"

"I haven't looked."

"Then what is troubling you."

Alistair walked over to a section of books and pulled out one of them. He opened it up to a certain page and handed it to Niro.

Niro read over the passage then slowly closed the book.

"The Larmat warriors drink the sacred juice when they earn the right to become warrior. They can produce offspring anytime after that, but their females are less fertile so it takes them awhile to get pregnant. The Dascon females are very fertile and so any Larmat male that have sport with them can easily produce offspring. The talza root is given to the Dascon female right afterwards to ensure the abomination that may grow in her womb is destroyed."

"Alistair…" Niro didn't know what to say.

"Please don't look at me with pity…the reason I show you this is that the Dascon females who were rescued may have trouble producing offspring after been given that root so many times. Tomar should be advised."

"You are right. I will make sure to mention this to Tomar." Niro walked around the room just looking at the piles of books. "We could learn much about these people." Niro turned to Alistair. "You could learn much about your father."

"What if I don't wish to know?"

"It is your choice. But you would be a fool not to learn about your father. He must have been a great man to have such a love for your mother that he was willing to risk so much for her…and you. Now I am going to go back to my chamber. I am tired from my journey. We will talk more tomorrow."

Alistair nodded his head toward Niro. He sat down and looked at all the books in this room. Somewhere in these books lay his father's tale. Alistair looked at the book lying on the table. "Abomination," he whispered. Alistair pushed the book to the ground and stood up. He walked out of the vault and headed across the courtyard to the leader hut. He went to his chamber, but stopped as he reached the door. The most heavenly voice was singing a strange song. He never heard this song before but the female's voice brought calm to him. He leaned up against the door and just let her angel's voice encompass him.

After a few moments he slowly opened the door and there on the balcony was Anne, wearing a light blue dress. She was singing to the moon. This image burnt into Alistair's mind. Her basking in the moonlight, her beauty illuminated, her sweet melody dancing on the night air and that look of peace in her eyes. For the first time in a long time he felt serenity.

Anne stopped singing and just gazed out across the village.

"Please don't stop singing."

Anne quickly turned around startled by the sound of Alistair's voice.

"I didn't mean to frighten you."

"It's okay…I didn't realize you were there."

"Please sing again."

"I couldn't…I never sing in front of anyone." Anne walked into the chamber and to the other side of the room.

Alistair slowly moved toward her. "Please don't fear me." His voice was so gentle. He had to touch, had to taste her.

Anne couldn't move as Alistair got closer. His eyes, so warm…so beautiful…hypnotized her. His hand timidly reached out and lightly touched her shoulder.

"I want to claim the right to be your protector," he whispered as his hand trailed down her arm. He liked how his paler skin looked on her darker skin.

"I don't understand what that means."

"Let me…" He looked deeply into her eyes. "Let me have you. Let me proclaim to everyone that I have earned the right to be your protector." His eyes so filled with lust, but at the same time so vulnerable, silently pleading with her not to turn him away.

"I can't promise you anything." She wanted to tell him to leave, but she found herself unable to do so.

"All I want is the chance to prove I am worthy of you."

His words were sincere—she could see it in his eyes. Her body trembled as he pulled her into his arms.

"I won't hurt you." He forced himself to step away from her. She must give him permission to take her, even though it took all his will power to hold back. His body felt so alive with desire he was having trouble containing his lust.

Anne reached out her hand and timidly touched his hard muscular chest. He was so beautifully made, she wanted him badly. But…could she allow herself to be with him? Surely this would signify a much deeper meaning to him. She stepped back then reached for the tie that held her dress to her body. She couldn't refuse him, she should but she couldn't. Slowly her dress fell revealing her body to him.

"You are beyond beauty," he whispered. His body trembled just looking at her soft, curvy body. He removed his sword and untied his loincloth letting it fall to the floor.

Anne gasped seeing the size of his cock. He was surely going to stretch her to the point of pain.

"I will be gentle with you." Alistair moved closer. He lifted her up into his arms feeling her body tremble against his. He would have to control himself, though he wanted nothing more than to pin her under him and ride her until she screamed out his name. He carried her to the large bed and laid her gently down. He climbed onto the bed and slowly opened her legs. He needed to taste her. He lowered his head between her legs and buried his tongue into her pussy.

Anne reached down and grabbed his head letting his long soft hair fill her fingers. His tongue licked everywhere, the soft growling noise he made thrilled her. She could already feel her orgasm start to build.

"Yessss," she hissed as a powerful orgasm washed over her. His tongue eagerly lapped up her sweet nectar. Her body trembled as he pleasured her over and over with his eager tongue.

"AHHH!!" Alistair roared, lifting his head up from between her legs. "I must have you now." He grabbed her hips as he positioned himself between her legs then he drove his cock into her. He slowed his thrust when he saw the grimace on her face. "I am trying to be gentle," his voice was strained. His hands gripped her hips tighter as he tried to control his need to drive his cock hard into her over and over. "Let me be your protector," his soft deep voice pleaded.

"Alistair." Her pussy was so full, so stretched by his large cock. She was between pleasure and pain.

"Let me be your protector," he growled this time.

"Yes," she whispered, unable to deny him anything at this moment.

"Say it." His hands tightened up her hips as he slowly moved his cock in and out.

"I want you to be my protector," she said in a rush. She gasped when he pulled his cock out and flipped her over. He lifted her hips up and pushed her head back down. He rammed his cock into her, driving himself harder and faster into her.

The pleasure overwhelmed the discomfort of his large cock filling her. Her pussy grew wetter and wetter with each thrust of his cock. She tried to lift her head up but he pushed her back down. His roar filled the room sending shivers throughout her body. She moaned loudly with he bent over and bit her shoulder pinning her under him. He growled and grunted as he drove his cock faster and faster, deeper and harder until he arched up and cried out his pleasure. His cum came in streams over and over until his orgasm finally ebbed. Anne felt yet another powerful orgasm race through her body at the same time.

Alistair slowly pulled his cock from her and lay beside her. His hand gently stroked her back as she laid there enjoying the afterglow of her orgasm. "I swear I will prove myself worthy of you."

Anne couldn't say anything—she didn't really know what to say at this moment. She just laid there enjoying his tender caresses. She didn't want to think about what just happened. She only wanted to get lost in his caress.

ഇഇഇ

Anne woke up the next morning her body was a bit sore. Alistair made love to her several times the night before. He made her feel so desirable. His hunger for her seemed insatiable. She slowly sat up and saw a large bouquet of the most vibrant colored flowers she had ever seen before lying on his side of the bed. The fragrance of the flowers was intoxicating. She couldn't help but smile at this sweet gesture. She climbed out of bed and wrapped a covering around her. She gathered up the flowers and looked for something to put them in. She walked to the adjacent chamber.

"Wow, now that's a bath tub," she exclaimed, looking at the large bathing pool that was in the center of the room. A gentle steam rose up from the water.

"Alistair has instructed me to help you bathe," a woman's voice startled Anne.

"I didn't see you there," Anne said to the rather tall brunette.

"My name is Liza."

"I am Anne. It's nice to meet you."

"Would you like me to put those flowers in water for you?"

"Oh, yes please."

Liza grabbed a long crystal looking vase and then walked over to the bathing pool. She filled the vase with some of the warm water from the pool. Anne walked over to her and handed her the flowers.

"Alistair chose these flowers himself for you. Of course any Dascon male would think to do such a nice gesture."

"I take it that the Larmat male wouldn't."

"No…not any I had the displeasure of knowing. I find it hard to believe Alistair has their vile blood in his veins. He is too kind to be part of these people." Liza set the flowers up on a stone mantel. "Now let's get you bathed."

"I would rather bathe myself. If you could just bring me what I need I would appreciate it."

"Alright." Liza gathered up a few things and handed the items over to Anne. "The bathing bar will clean everything. If you need anything else I will be in your chamber getting your covering ready."

"Thank you."

When Liza left the room Anne removed her covering then slowly stepped into the warm water of the bath. She sat down so that the water went up to her neck. The warm water felt so good on her sore body. Her mind drifted as she let the water soothed her. There had to be some good to these Larmat people. Perhaps prejudice had clouded the minds of the Dascon people.

"Oh…this is so surreal. Maybe this is…all this is…a dream. Taken to a strange planet…a planet full of hot men, warring clans and women treated like either precious gems or sex slaves. This all sounds like a plot to a romance novel." She started to chuckle. "But this is reality girl." She closed her eyes and tried to absorb everything. Even through her cluttered thoughts she couldn't get Alistair's pale blue eyes out of her mind. If the eyes are the window to the soul, then his eyes showed so much. Loving, caring, but oh so vulnerable…and warmth, even a deep sadness, his eyes showed all of this.

She reached up and grabbed the bathing bar. It had a nice fragrance to it. She began washing herself then lathered up her hair. Her thoughts wouldn't leave her. Thoughts of him wouldn't leave her. She ducked under the water to rinse off her hair. When she surfaced she saw a pair of strong legs. She quickly covered her breasts.

"You shouldn't hide your beautiful body."

She let out a sigh of relief hearing Alistair's voice.

"Thank you for the flowers. They were lovely."

"I am glad you liked them." He removed his loincloth and slowly climbed into the bath. He went under water and slowly emerged right next to her. His long light brown hair clung to his back. Anne couldn't take her eyes off of him.

He smiled then grabbed her arms and held them down on the rim of the bath.

"I had to feel your body again," he purred as he pressed his body against hers.

She wrapped her legs around his waist and pulled him closer.

"I see you desire my body as well." He smiled so sexily as he rubbed his cock against her pussy, teasing her. Her sweet moan was music to his ears as he let his cock stroke her clit. He watched her face as she closed her eyes and enjoyed the sensations he brought to her.

"Look at me," he whispered. The second her eyes fluttered open and locked with his, he drove his cock into her.

"Oh…ssss…" she moaned.

"Keep looking at me." He watched the pleasure build, he wanted to see the moment she orgasmed. He fought to control himself—he wouldn't come before she had her pleasure. His thrusts were steady and firm as he continued to watch her.

"Let me see your pleasure," he whispered.

Anne tried to keep her eyes open as her orgasm washed over her. "Let me see your pleasure," she said seductively.

Alistair couldn't stop his orgasm. He roared loudly and threw his head back as he came. The intensity of his orgasm caused his body to shudder. He released her hands then moved his hands to her wet hair. He gently stroked her face and hair. She took pleasure being with him, he saw no disgust or shame in her eyes. She wanted to be with him, not out of duty, but because she wanted him.

"What's wrong?" Anne said, bringing her hands to his face.

"Nothing." He smiled. He enjoyed her sweet caresses for a few more moments then he pulled away from her. "I have to meet with Niro this morning. What would you like to do? Whatever you want I will make it possible." Alistair climbed out of the bath and dried himself off then put his loincloth back on.

"I would like to explore this village if that is okay."

"If this is what you would like to do I will provide an escort for you. But promise me that you will not wander out of the village and that you will stay with your escort."

"I promise."

His smile lit up his face. "I will send your escort in about an hour." He squatted down and ran his hand over her head. "If you need me I will be in the meeting room or training grounds. Your escort will know where each of these areas is."

"Okay." She smiled up at him. It was strange, but she felt safe with him almost as if she had known him forever.

Alistair stood up and left the room. Anne climbed out of the bath and dried herself off. She had to get ready. She was eager to explore this village.

After about an hour Anne heard a loud knock on the door. This had to be the escort Alistair said he was going to provide. She knew this escort was here to protect her, whoever it was. She wasn't really afraid. She only hoped he was at least somewhat friendly.

Anne opened the door and was rather relieved to see Demos.

"Hello Demos."

"Alistair wanted me to escort you around the village. A Dascon female will also be joining us so she can tell you about the village. I hope you will refrain from throwing objects at me."

"What…oh…ummm…where is Nina?"

"She is guarding Robin and Zenos."

"She is?" Anne was surprised by this. Nina had to be the only female warrior on Malka.

"Of course, she has trained with me and has earned the rights of a warrior."

"Nina is the only female warrior isn't she?" Anne couldn't help but smile at the look of pride that swept over Demos' face.

"Yes, my flower is the only female warrior. Are you ready to go?"

"Yes, lead the way."

Anne followed Demos out of the chamber. She smiled seeing Liza waiting for them just outside.

"Great Demos." Liza bowed her head to him. "Hello again, Anne."

"I am excited to see this village. I am glad you are the one who will be showing me everything."

"It's my pleasure. But remember don't wander off without Demos."

"I won't."

Liza led her first over to the stables, inside were all sorts of conjas.

"Oh I remember these creatures." Anne walked over to Susie. "Especially you, girl." She slowly reached out her hand.

"Be careful," Demos said.

Anne slowly petted Susie's scaly skin. "These creatures are fascinating. Back on Earth I was training to be a vet. Mostly small animals though."

"Vet?" Demos asked.

Anne turned to him. "An animal doctor…healer."

"Healer…of animals. This skill is needed in Dascon and probably here in Larmat too," Demos said.

"You were allowed to train?" Liza asked.

"Things are a bit different on Earth than they are here."

"You should speak with Tomar he has a couple of animal healers in his clan. Perhaps you can continue your training…if Alistair doesn't have a problem with that," Demos said.

"I am looking forward to meeting with Tomar."

Anne followed Liza through the stables then up to the history vault. "Inside this hut is the record of the Larmat clan."

"Can we go in?"

"Only if Alistair gives you permission to."

"Okay." Anne followed Liza over to the weapon maker area. Anne watched as these strong men forged swords, spears, knives and other weapons from the hot steel. The rhythmic pounding of the hammers against the steel made its own music.

Liza led Anne to a cluster of huts. "This is where the slaves were held." Liza looked back at Demos. She hoped Demos wouldn't grow angry. These buildings were used to house the Dascon females that were stolen from their villages. Liza lived in one of these huts while she was a prisoner. She had blocked out most of her ordeal. The only really clear memory is when Alistair set all of the Dascon females free, right after he was proclaimed leader of the Larmat.

"Were held?" Anne asked.

"Alistair freed all the females. Now these huts are used for travelers."

Anne followed Liza around all afternoon. The village was rather large. She saw the larger more impressive huts of the older retired warriors. She was pleased that this society honored its old. She leisurely went through the market area. She saw where females and children lived and where the warriors were housed.

"Why are the females and males housed separately?"

"Unlike Dascon where males and females become mates, here most males don't have mates. They simply just take females when they want. If a warrior favors a particular female he will let her live with him so that he can keep the other warriors away from her. But once he tires of her she is sent back to live with the other females. Often this is when she has a child. Larmat males don't care for their offspring the way Dascon males do."

"How can these two clans be so different?"

"Larmat males are just animals," Liza said quietly.

"Not all of them can be this way."

"The ones I have seen are."

"Let's keep moving," Demos said. His eyes quickly went to the large Larmat warrior that entered the village. This warrior was easily six foot eight; his long golden blond hair was tied back. Demos never seen this warrior before, but he hasn't been here long enough to memorize all of the Larmat warriors who occupied the village.

Ivor looked over the village. He was disgusted to see so many Dascon warriors in the main village. They had no right to be here. Damn Rasmus for losing to Niro. Ivor stopped when he saw the dark-skinned female. Who was this vision? He wanted to go over there and take this new female, but stopped when he saw she was being guarded by Demos. That mark over one of Demos' eyes, every Larmat warrior knew about Demos. He was the one who killed Rasmus, was the one who saved Niro from Malin. If a grand warrior such as he was guarding this female she must be either Niro or Alistair's mate. Ivor made a mental note of this.

Anne saw the large blond warrior staring at her. She felt Demos move closer to her. Soon the warrior moved on. She didn't like the way that warrior looked at her.

"Now I will show you the training grounds," Liza said.

Anne decided not to worry about the warrior. If something was wrong she was sure Demos would have done something.

They headed over to the training grounds. The sound of swords clashing filled the air.

"Alistair and Niro," Liza said.

Anne saw the way Liza lit up and wondered if it was Alistair or Niro that excited Liza. Anne watched as Alistair and Niro sparred.

"I have heard much about Niro, but I have never seen him before. He is magnificent."

Anne was strangely relieved that it was Niro who was drawing so much excitement from Liza and not Alistair. "Are they going to hurt each other?" Anne asked as she watched the intensity in which the two sparred.

"No, both are well trained," Demos said.

Anne couldn't take her eyes away from the two men. Both were very skilled and their sparring match started to look like a deadly dance to her. After a little while both men stopped, both looked tired.

Alistair shook Niro's hand. "Good fight."

"Same to you, Alistair, I see I will have to keep training to keep up with you." Niro looked over to Demos and the two females. "It seems as though your female has come to watch you."

Alistair quickly glanced over to where Niro was looking. Alistair couldn't help but smile at Anne. He walked over to her. "Are you enjoying your tour of the village?" he asked as he came up to her.

"Very much so, Liza has been very helpful with showing me around."

Alistair smiled at Liza. He had taken Liza as one of his females to protect her from the other warriors. She was too ashamed to go back to her village when he freed the other females. She asked if she could stay with him. He knew she had been used several times by various Larmat warriors during her captivity. So, he kept her in a chamber next to his. He was going to find her a Dascon protector, but since she was used by so many Larmat warriors finding her a protector was proving to be challenging.

"I will join you later I must head back to Niro." Alistair reached out his hand and gently caressed her hair. Alistair nodded his head to Demos then headed back to Niro.

"We must head back to the leader hut," Demos said.

"Is it alright to visit with Robin for a little while?" Anne asked. Anne liked being with Robin. It made her feel better. Perhaps it was because Robin was once from Earth or maybe it was the gentleness that surrounded Robin. Either way Anne felt more at ease with her.

"I don't see why not."

Demos let the two women go on ahead as he followed them. Something about that large warrior he saw entering the village didn't sit right with him. He would have to bring this up with Alistair later.

Chapter Six

Anne enjoyed her visit with Robin. Demos escorted her back to Alistair's chamber. Demos left shortly afterwards. Anne sat down on the bed. She was tired from the day's activities. She wanted to go into the history vault and read about the Larmat people. There had to be something good about these people.

She sat up at the head of the bed and wrapped her arms around her legs, laying her cheek against her knees. Thoughts of her parents flooded her mind. The brief time she has spent with Alistair allowed her to forget the pain of losing them. Now guilt mixed with her sadness. How could she forget even for a moment? She had to focus on getting the people responsible for taking her parents' lives. But how being here? For a year now everyday was dedicated to that goal. She worked then went home and worked on the case on her own and with the police. Now…

Alistair stood out on the balcony just watching her. He didn't want to disturb her when Demos brought her back. He was enjoying just looking at her, but this sadness that washed over her tore at him.

♪*Some say love it is a river…that drowns the tender reed. Some say love is a razor that leads your soul to bleed. Some say love is a hunger, an endless aching need. I say love it is a flower and you its only seed.* ♪

Alistair slowly walked over to Anne as she continued to sing to herself.

♪*When the night has been too lonely and the road has been too long.* ♪

He came down to his knees before the bed. She slowly looked up and saw him.

♪*And you think that love is only for the lucky and the strong*♪

She moved over to him. She sat up placing her legs on each side of him. She opened her arms and he fell into them. She held him tightly to her.

♪*Just remember in the winter far beneath the bitter snow. Lies the seed that with the sun's love in the spring becomes the rose.*♪

She held him so tightly to her as the tears escaped. Alistair wrapped his strong arms even tighter around her. "Tell me what's wrong? Let me help you," he whispered.

"How could I forget? How?" she sobbed.

"Forgot what? Please let me try to help you."

"My parents were murdered a year ago. The people who did this were never caught. I have been trying to catch their murderers…" she said in a rush. She felt Alistair hold her tighter. "When I am with you I forgot about them. I can't forget I have to…" She sobbed uncontrollably now.

"It is okay. Sometimes you must allow yourself to forget."

"No…it's wrong…"

"Anne, no it isn't."

"You don't know what I am talking about."

"Yes, I do in a way. My father disappeared and mother would have been forced into exile if it wasn't for Hakan…"

"Alistair…" She released him and looked into his face. "Oh Alistair I am sorry that was so insensitive of me."

"You needn't apologize." He cupped her face in his hands. "I can't dwell on all the cruelties that have been inflicted on me. I won't. If I do the people who call me half- breed or worse an abomination win, their cruelty wins and I won't let that happen. Your parents wouldn't want you to wallow in misery all the time. Their murderers will face justice in this life or the next, you losing your ability to live will not hasten this."

"But it would be as if I stop caring about them…"

"No Anne, your parents will always live in your heart, the way my mother will always live in mine."

"What about your father?"

"I never really knew my father."

Anne started to cry again. All the emotions she had bottled up since her parents' death bubbled up to the surface. Alistair pulled her back into his arms and held her tightly. "Cry Anne, let it all out."

Anne cried and cried until she fell asleep in his embrace.

ლჍჂ

Anne woke up the next morning and Alistair was gone. He held her so close all night, she felt so safe lying there with him like that.

She got ready and was greeted by Nina.

"Good morning Anne, Alistair wants you to follow me."

"Good morning Nina." Anne followed Nina to outside of the history vault. A group of older women were standing there.

"Anne," Alistair's deep quiet voice called out.

Anne smiled at him as he walked over to her.

"What's going on?" she asked, looking at the older women.

"I have caught you singing twice now. So…you must love music."

"Yes, I love music. But I don't see what that has to do with…"

"Listen." He gestured to the older women. Half of them reached behind and grabbed strange looking string instruments. As soon as they were ready they begin playing the other half started to sing a most beautiful melody. It sounded like what a mother might sing to her child.

Anne closed her eyes and let the music wash over her. She couldn't stop herself from swaying gently to the soft melody. Alistair smiled watching Anne enjoy the music.

"This song is beautiful."

"It is the song my mother always sang to me."

When the women finished Anne clapped her hands. "Very nice," she said to the women.

"These women know many Larmat songs and I can have singers brought from Dascon too if you would like."

"That song was a Larmat song?"

"Yes, mother said it was the same song my father's mother sang to him. She said he sang this same song to me when I was a baby. Anytime you wish I can have these women make music for you."

"That's so sweet Alistair, thank you."

"Now I wish I could spend all day with you, but I still have much to discuss with Niro."

"Oh that's okay, you go do what you have to do."

"Liza told me that you were interested in reading about the Larmat people. You can go into the history vault and read what you wish. I am not sure if you can read their words or not, I can provide a translator if you need. But please stay with Nina."

"Alright."

Alistair pulled her into his arms and kissed her so passionately she thought she might melt right there. "My body aches for yours," he whispered in her ear. "If only I had time to have you." He nibbled on her ear then released her. He bowed his head to the older women then quickly walked away.

"Whoa, I could feel the heat you two generated all the way over here," Nina teased her.

"Umm, let's go into the history vault." Anne wanted to change the subject.

"Alright…lead the way."

Anne looked around in amazement of the sheer volume of books that were inside the vault. She grabbed one of the books gently and opened the pages. The writing was very similar to English.

"Amazing isn't it, how their written word is so similar to ours. The Dascon writing is a bit more of a challenge to read. Luckily I have Demos to translate for me," Nina said.

"It is amazing. I think I can piece together what is written here."

"Well I will leave you to it." Nina went over to the door and sat down next to it.

Anne spent the afternoon pouring over the pages of several books. Mostly what she found was books on family history. Offspring were always called the son of male warriors, Talb son of Daemon, etc etc. This did little to help Anne understand much.

Anne walked over to one of the older women who was writing something in a book. All the books here were hand written.

"Excuse me, are there any books about Alistair's father."

"Tibor…" the older woman quietly said. She stood up and walked back to a row of shelves and pulled one of the books off of it. She walked back to Anne and handed her the book.

"Thank you." Anne carried the book back to her seat and slowly opened it. It was strange that Alistair said he knew little about his father. He could have easily read this very book and learned. Why didn't he?

Anne read what a grand warrior Tibor was, second only to the guards of the ruler of Larmat. She read about his countless victories and the many females given to him. Tibor however had no Larmat children. If he did they weren't mention. Anne gasped when she read the header to the next passage, *The Fall of Tibor.*

He was sentence to death for helping a Dascon female escape, but will be forever shamed for allowing the Dascon woman to bear his child. Anne's heart ached as she read the transcripts of Tibor's trial. He refused to tell where his son was. They offered to spare his life and to lower his punishment to exile to a far off village if he told them where the child was. Tibor still refused. They wouldn't allow the abomination created by Tibor and the Dascon female to be named during the trial. Upon hearing those words Tibor cried out his son's name...Alistair. Tibor drew his sword and attacked his fellow warriors. He was vastly outnumbered and was taken down, his execution was made public. He died a very painful death, but never did he tell them where his son could be found. Anne read the last page that looked to be recently added. It was rumored that it was Tibor who asked the Dascon leader Hakan to take pity on his Dascon mate Pedita and their child Alistair. Hakan was touched that the warrior that swore to kill every last Dascon warrior could humble himself before the leader of his enemy to spare the life of his mate and child. Hakan promised Tibor that the female and child would be safe. Tibor then returned to the Larmat village to receive his punishment.

"Alistair..." Anne whispered as she closed the book. "Nina."

"What's wrong?" Nina walked over to her.

"Alistair has to know what his father went through to keep him safe."

Nina sat down next to Anne. "Anne, if Alistair wanted to know about his father he would have read that book."

"Tibor saved Alistair's life. He went to Hakan to save them then he stood trial at this very Larmat village, he suffered an unimaginable death to save Alistair."

"You have to let Alistair decide when it's time to learn about his father."

"Alistair has to know just how much his father loved him."

"Excuse me," an older woman walked over to them. "Alistair has requested that Anne be brought to the feasting hall."

"Alright," Nina said. "Anne, leave the book for now."

Anne slowly sat the book down. She knew Nina was right this was something Alistair had to do on his own.

"I don't know about you but I am starving. Oh…you are going to like this. I heard that Tomar is arriving. Perhaps he is already here and that is why we have to go to the feasting hall."

"The lizard people's leader?"

"Yep, they really do look like lizards so prepare yourself."

"I think it would be cool to see something like that."

"You are braver than I was. I remember seeing a Rundal for the first time—they kind of freaked me out a little."

Anne followed Nina out of the history vault. Nina quickly pulled her sword out and placed herself in front of Anne.

"What's going on?" Anne froze when she saw the large blond warrior from earlier.

"So you are Demos' mate…ppphh…a female warrior how ridiculous."

"Step back. Who are you anyways?"

"I saw this warrior earlier," Anne whispered to Nina.

"I am Ivor, a Larmat warrior…I belong in this village you do not." Ivor looked at Anne and smiled. "I want that female behind you, so step aside Dascon female warrior."

"You step any closer and I will hurt you. Alistair is this female's protector."

"What is your strange custom, oh yes if I want this female I must challenge Alistair for her."

"That's right."

"Where is Alistair?"

"He has left this female in my care for now."

"So that means I have to challenge you?"

"No, that means back the fuck off unless you want me to hurt you."

Ivor started to laugh. He quickly turned around when he heard a sword being drawn.

"You dare speak to my mate," Demos growled.

"You are in a Larmat village Dascon scum, your customs mean nothing here."

"Demos…" Nina placed her sword back into its scabbard. "I have to take Anne to the feasting chamber we don't have time to deal with this asshole." Nina hoped that by sheathing her sword the other two would do the same. To her relief they did.

"I will challenge Alistair for that female." Ivor smiled at Anne again then turned and left.

"Demos, I have never seen that particular warrior before."

"I had him checked out, he is from some remote village. No doubt he wants to try and become a warrior for this main village."

"Why...all warriors in the Dascon clan are looked upon with the same respect regardless of what village they come from."

"It doesn't work that way here. We will have to keep our eye on that warrior."

"I am glad you showed up." Nina smiled at him.

"Alistair wants to see Anne. Tomar has arrived."

"Told you," Nina said to Anne.

"I am proud how you handle such a large warrior, my flower."

Nina loved when Demos had that look of pride and love in his eyes. She had trained so hard to be the best warrior she could to bring him this kind of pride.

"We must hurry." Demos gently caressed Nina's hair.

Anne liked watching these two together. They were so in love and it showed. She followed them toward the feasting hall. She was most eager to see what a Rundal looked like.

Alistair quickly came to his feet when he saw Anne entering the hall. He wanted to hurry over to her in case she was afraid of the Rundals. He started to move over to her then stopped when Anne just walked right up to one of the Rundal guards and touched him.

Anne let her hand go down the rubbery, scaly black skin of the Rundal guard. She smiled up at the large male. "I am sorry I shouldn't have just walked up and touched you like that."

"I don't mind, but your barbarian male might have a problem with it."

"How are you talking without moving your mouth?" Anne studied the reptilian face of the guard.

"We use our minds to communicate."

Anne turned toward the gentle voice that spoke. She let her eyes wander over the large Rundal male.

"I am Tomar."

"Oh…it is an honor to meet you." She grabbed Tomar's claw and gently shook it. His claw felt soft almost like a human's hands. Anne started examining Tomar's hand.

"Well look at that," Nina said to Demos. "She isn't afraid of the Rundals at all—she seems more fascinated with them." Nina looked up at Demos, she could see the confuse look on his face.

"Perhaps I should make her stop touching them like that?" Demos quietly said.

"If Alistair or the Rundals don't have a problem with it then we should just let her be."

Anne walked over to a female Rundal. She let her hand slowly go down the female's green rubbery skin. The females skin was much softer than the males was.

"I am Sasha, Tomar's mate," Sasha said with amusement in her voice.

"Nice to meet you, Sasha. May I touch your tail?"

"Go ahead."

Anne walked behind Sasha and gently let her hand wander down Sasha's long thin tail. She was amazed how soft it felt.

"What do you eat? Do you have the same laws and customs as the barbarians?" Anne asked as she walked back to the front of the reptilian couple.

"Your curiosity is most flattering," Tomar said.

Anne walked behind Tomar and let her hand caress his much thicker tale.

"Anne." Alistair's soft deep voice caught her attention.

"Oh…I am sorry I hope I'm not being rude." Anne moved over to Alistair.

"I am just surprised that you are not frightened by the Rundals." Alistair wrapped his arm protectively around Anne. He didn't really like the way she kept touching the male Rundal, especially when she caressed Tomar's tail that way. The Rundal's tail is one of their erogenous zones. Of course Anne had no idea what she was doing and Tomar and Sasha was being most gracious allowing her to sate her curiosity.

"Your female is most curious," Tomar said. He could sense Alistair's uneasiness. The last thing he wanted was a barbarian warrior's anger.

"I have crossed some sort of etiquette line haven't I? I am sorry…it's just I have never seen anything like the Rundals before."

Alistair reached up his hand and gently stroked her hair. He looked around the room and could see the shocked looks on all the warriors in the room. "It is okay. Please let's sit and enjoy the feast that has been prepared in Tomar's honor." Alistair gestured for Tomar and Sasha to be seated. He escorted Anne to the seat next to his.

"Tell me what I did?" Anne whispered.

Alistair motioned for the feast to begin then sat down. He grabbed Anne's hand and placed it on his hard cock. He moved her hand up and down on his cloth-covered cock a few times. "This is what you did to Tomar."

"What?!"

"When you caress his tail he can feel much pleasure."

"Oh…I am so embarrassed." She tried to move her hand from his cock but he held her hand to him.

"I need you," he whispered in her ear.

"Right here?" She looked around the room and saw that her earlier faux pas seemed to be forgotten.

Alistair released her hand then stood up. "Come with me," he whispered.

"But…"

She stood up and followed him to a room that was just off to the side. Alistair closed the curtain then lunged for her. He lifted her up with one arm and quickly undid his loincloth with the other hand.

Anne wrapped her legs around him as he pulled up her covering.

"Alistair," she moaned when he impaled her with his huge cock. "Somebody might come in or hear us."

"Ahhhh…" he groaned as he drove his cock harder and deeper into her. "I have been thinking about your body all day."

"Harder Alistair, harder, harder…Harder!" She didn't care anymore that someone might hear them. His hunger for her and the sweet pleasure he was giving her drowned out any sense of modesty.

"Rrrrrr!" Alistair growled as he drove his cock harder and harder into her, her ass pounding against the wall with each powerful thrust.

"Yessss Alistair," she purred.

"I want all of my cock into you…but I don't want to hurt you." He tightened his hold on her hips trying to control himself.

"Fill me Alistair, oh God fill me."

With one powerful thrust he buried his cock to the hilt in her. He paused only for a moment to make sure he wasn't hurting her. When he saw the look of absolute bliss on her face, he drove his cock harder and faster into her, burying himself to the hilt with each stroke.

"I am going to come…oh Alistair don't stop, oh please don't stop." She tightened her hold on him as her orgasm built and built. When her orgasm crescendo she bit her lip to stop herself from screaming his name. He kept on thrusting, harder and harder, deeper and faster causing her to climax again. This time she couldn't squelch her cries of desire.

"ALISTAIR!!!" she cried out.

"Yessss, my female....oh my female let them hear your pleasure." He thrust faster and faster feeling his orgasm start to build. He roared as his orgasm washed over him. He buried his cock to the hilt in her as his seed filled her. He pressed her against the wall with his body as he enjoyed the afterglow of his orgasm. "My female." He nuzzled his head against hers. "My female," he purred.

Reluctantly he released her and gently set her back down. "We must rejoin the feast." He softly caressed her cheek.

"I have to go clean up first."

"Go straight down and there will be a bathing chamber, please hurry back to the feasting hall."

Anne raised her hands and pulled his head down to her. She softly kissed his lips. "I will hurry." She released him and headed out the back way of the room.

Alistair watched her until she was out of sight. He took a deep breath then walked back into the feasting hall.

Anne finished cleaning herself up then lightly chuckled to herself when she realized what she did earlier. "Masturbating a reptile man right there in front of everyone, oh boy... I wonder if reptile men have cocks." The Rundals were wearing clothing. She was most curious now. "Or how they make love. Alright girl, that's enough of that line of thinking." She checked herself in the mirror. She could still smell Alistair's scent on her skin—still hear his grunts and moans in her mind. Her body became aroused just thinking about the hungry way he just took her. She had to hurry up and get back to the feast she knew Alistair would start worrying about her soon.

Anne walked out of the bathing chamber and was immediately lifted off her feet. "Alistair…"

"I am not that half-breed," Ivor growled.

"Oh my God, put me down…damn it put me down."

"I want to bury my cock in you."

"No…no…"She pounded hard against his back as he pinned her to the wall.

"You let that half-breed stick his cock into you. You should feel honored that I still want you after he has soiled you."

"Alistair!" she cried. "Alistair!!" She struggled hard, but Ivor was too strong. He tore at her covering. The next instant she felt herself fall to the ground. Dazed she slowly looked up when she heard swords being unsheathed.

"You dare touch my female," Alistair growled.

"You know the Larmat traditions. Any female not guarded by a male can be taken by any warrior who wants her."

"I am her protector and it is Dascon tradition to slay you for touching her."

"You are in a Larmat village half-breed," Ivor growled.

"AHHHRRR!!!" Alistair cried out as he attacked Ivor.

"Alistair…" Anne slowly stood up. She couldn't let him do this. He may get killed. "Alistair please stop!" she yelled.

"Are you alright?" Nina hurried over to Anne.

"Please make Alistair stop."

"He is your protector. He will kill any male that harms you," Demos said.

"I don't want him to kill anyone. Please…I am begging you to make him stop."

Nina hurried over to Alistair, which made Demos immediately rush after her. Demos blocked Ivor's sword making Alistair step back.

"What are you doing? This male touched my female," Alistair growled.

"Your female needs you," Nina said.

Alistair looked behind him and saw Anne standing there in her ripped covering. His anger swelled, he was just about to push Demos out of the way and attack Ivor again.

"Alistair please stop," Anne's voice pleaded.

Alistair sheathed his sword and rushed over to her. Anne latched onto him.

"Leave this village and never return. The next time I see you I will kill you," Alistair growled to Ivor.

"You allow your female to tell you what to do…pathetic." Ivor spat in the direction of Alistair was. "You will not rule my people, you dirty half-breed. This peace between the Larmat and Dascon will be short lived."

"Stop calling him that!" Anne stepped out of Alistair's embrace.

Alistair immediately grabbed her and placed her behind him. "Go now Ivor or I will have you executed now."

"Your female…will be mine Alistair."

"Go!" Demos growled as he raised his sword to Ivor's neck.

Ivor turned around and walked away. Demos followed him to make sure he left the village.

"Are you alright? Did he…" Alistair cupped her face in his hand.

"I am okay and no he didn't rape me."

"I should have never left you alone…I have failed you."

"No you haven't please don't say that."

"Why did you stop me? Ivor should be dead for what he has done to you."

"I couldn't bear to see you hurt."

"You don't think I could have defeat Ivor?" Alistair had such a wounded look on his face it tore at Anne.

"I am sure you could have…it's just that I didn't want to see you get hurt."

"Ivor should have died."

"I don't want someone to die because of me. Punished yes, but you don't have to kill him."

"You wish for me to spare Ivor's life…is this why you stopped me?"

Anne saw the anger and hurt seep into Alistair's eyes.

"Oh damn it…I am saying this wrong." She looked over to Nina.

"Alistair, I think she is trying to say you are the better warrior and she didn't want any blood being spilt for you to prove that. She already knows you are."

Anne was relieved to see Alistair's eyes light up.

"Is this what you are trying to say?"

"Yes Alistair." She couldn't help but smile seeing his face lit up and that beautiful smile of his.

"Let me help Anne get another covering on," Nina said.

"I should go with her."

"Alistair you can't leave Niro and Tomar in the feasting hall by themselves. I promise I won't let her out of my sight."

"Alright, but hurry."

Alistair caressed Anne's hair. "Are you sure you are alright?"

"I am fine now."

"Don't let her out of your sight."

Nina nodded her head to Alistair then escorted Anne back to her chamber. She sat on the bed while Anne quickly changed her clothes. "The one main thing to remember is that the males on this planet must feel like they are best warriors. Battle prowess is the all important to them. You can never make your male feel like he is second to any warrior in your eyes. I know this is a bit silly at times, but it is how this world works."

"I want to thank you for clearing that up with Alistair. I had no idea what I was doing was wrong."

"The male ego is very fragile on this planet."

"Do you need to feel like you are the best warrior?"

Nina started laughing. "No, I don't need to have Demos telling me I am the best warrior. Since I am the first female warrior most of these males don't know how to act around me."

"Do you have to reassure Demos all the time?"

"Demos is the best warrior in my eyes. He trained me and he made it possible for me to be a warrior too. Though between you and me…sometimes we spar to see who will be in charge in the bedroom."

"Oh…." Anne started to laugh.

"Most of the time Demos wins, but I like it when he is dominant in the bedroom. He can get so animal like."

"Alistair is so animal like too. Can I ask you something? It's kind of personal."

"Go ahead."

"When Alistair claimed me as his…you know…female…the way he pinned me under him and took me so animal like was so hot…especially when he bit my shoulder to keep me pinned under him. Did Demos do this to you?"

"Oh God yes…I just love it when he does that."

"So if I want Alistair to do that again…"

"The way to get him to do that again is to position yourself like you wanted it doggy style then just tell Alistair he is your male. This gets them all worked up. Make sure you purr at him that he is your male. I guarantee he will be biting your shoulder and giving you the ride of your life."

"I will have to try that. Nina…"

"Please feel free to talk to me about anything."

"Do you feel like you belong to Demos, that you were meant to be with him, especially when you just started being together? And is it wrong to feel like this when I have obligations back on Earth?"

"I gave Demos a pretty hard time when we first got together. I didn't want to belong to any man. But…I realized that I did belong here with Demos. He is everything to me and I couldn't picture my life without him. Your obligations on Earth can wait. Niro said the Rundal ship was going back in six months. I am sure Alistair would want you to fulfill those obligations, just talk to him. He loves you I can see it in his eyes."

"How can he love me already?"

"When these big lugs fall in love they don't waste time."

Anne adjusted her covering. "I am still shaking. Ivor was going to rape me."

"That is why it is very important that you never go anywhere without your protector or an escort that he has provided. Especially here in the Larmat village where women are just looked upon like objects or trophies. Alistair is trying to change this, but it will take time."

Anne sat down on the bed next to Nina. "Thank you for talking with me. You know you can talk to me too, if you need to."

"I will remember that. Now let's get you back to the feasting hall before Alistair tears this place apart looking for you."

Anne smiled at Alistair when they entered the feasting hall. That look of relief on his face warmed her heart. He stood as she approached and pulled out her chair for her.

"Sorry I took so long," she said as she sat down.

"I was about to go out and find you."

"Nina was with me."

"That was the only reason I didn't."

Anne looked around and saw Nina sitting down next to Demos. She glanced over at Niro and Robin, then Tomar and Sasha. The large room was filled with Dascon and Larmat warriors.

"Niro tells me you are a healer of animals," Tomar said.

"I was training to be an animal doctor back on Earth."

"There are so few animal healers here on Malka, perhaps I could persuade Alistair to let you train with me."

"Tomar is an excellent healer of Rundals, barbarians and animals," Sasha added.

"Would you like that?" Alistair asked.

"Yes I would."

Alistair watched Anne talk with Tomar, the way her face lit up as they discuss animal healing. She fascinated Tomar Alistair could see that as well.

"Your female has much in common with Tomar," Niro said as the dinner was being served.

"It looks that way."

"Then you should allow her to study with him. It is a great honor."

"I know...but..."

"Alistair, you must focus on joining the clans. What Demos has told me about Ivor…he targeted your female."

"He hates having a half-breed lead his people."

"Demos thinks there was more to it than that. He believes Ivor was a spy."

"Spy?"

"The rumors of rebels forming must be true." Niro watched Alistair stare at Anne as she continued talking with Tomar. "Alistair, I am sorry but you can't let your female distract you from your goal. Alistair…"

Alistair turned to Niro.

"I will send half of all Dascon warriors down here to force the Larmat to adapt. I will not chance the Larmat warriors forming a large force and attacking Dascon. This is why I am here to see how far you have come to helping me join the two clans."

"I know…I am sorry Niro. I will send warriors out to search the villages for any sign of a rebellion and I will have them kill the Larmat warriors who wish to revolt."

"I have already sent several warriors to search each village."

"What?"

"You have more pressing issues. You have to convince the Larmat people that we wish them no harm, that both clans can live in peace."

"They can't see beyond who I am."

"You are the son of the great Larmat warrior Tibor." Niro motioned to a weaker male. "Go get that book I showed you earlier from my chamber," Niro said to the small male.

"Yes Niro."

"You shouldn't have brought him. Larmat despise the thought of using weaker males."

"Robin wanted to bring Laigne with us. He is her favorite weaker male."

"Still."

"I give my female whatever she wants. I am sure you can understand that now."

"Yes…I would give Anne anything she wanted."

"Then let her train with Tomar. Look at her…"

Alistair looked over Anne again. She was enjoying her conversation with Tomar. Alistair could fell a pang of jealousy. But Niro was right she would love to train with Tomar.

"Tomar, I would be honored for you to train Anne."

"Thank you Alistair."

"Really…" She smiled at him. "But what about what you need to do. Surely I can help you somehow."

"Training with Tomar will make you happy. I can take care of what I need to do. Besides it will give you something to do while I am busy."

"Alistair." Niro handed Alistair a book. "Read this."

"What is it?"

"A book my father had written for you. He wanted to wait until you were ready. He died before he had the chance to give it to you. Robin found this while she was helping me organize all of father's writings to give to the Dascon history vault."

"Hakan wrote this for me?" Alistair lovingly caressed the leather cover.

"Yes, when you are ready read it."

Anne looked over at Alistair. She watched him lightly caress a cover of a book then he motioned for a female to come over to him. "Take this to my chamber and set it on my desk."

"Yes Alistair."

"What was that?" Anne asked.

"A gift from Hakan."

Anne placed her hand on his leg and gently squeezed. She knew in that book contained the real truth about Alistair's father, it had to be. After what she read about Tibor from the Larmat history vaults he sounded like a great man. Would Alistair read the book? She felt his large hand cover her hand on his thigh. He gave her hand a gentle squeeze.

Chapter Seven

Rodan managed to get his warriors out of the village of Exoida before Niro's warriors arrived. He had anticipated such a move from Niro and was rather pleased that the leader of the Dascon clan wasn't a fool. It would make Rodan's victory all that much sweeter. His only fear was that his brother Ivor would fail in his mission to bring Niro or Alistair's mate to him. He didn't want to wait much longer to attack the main Larmat village. Niro was too smart a warrior to leave the main village of Dascon unguarded. Their only hope was to regain control of the main Larmat village. This would encourage the other Larmat warriors to join them in their revolt.

"Don't fail me Ivor," Rodan whispered as he looked over his warriors. Each one of them was ready.

ജ്ഞ

Anne waited in Alistair's chamber. Alistair was meeting with Niro again and would be back soon.

She removed her covering and sat down on the bed. She felt a little nervous about taking charge of their lovemaking, but she craved for Alistair to take her like an animal. She couldn't stop thinking about it. The feel of his large body covering hers, the sounds he made as he bit her shoulder…her body shuddered just thinking about it.

She jerked when she heard the chamber door open. She slowly looked up and saw Alistair just staring at her naked body. That look on his face fanned the flames of her desire to a raging inferno. He slowly walked over to her, kicking the door shut behind him. He quickly removed his sword, then his loincloth.

"Wait," she quietly said.

"I can't wait. I want you…now."

"Alistair," she purred his name making him lunge for her. "Wait…" She gently pushed on his large body.

He rolled off of her. His breathing was labored as he tried to control his urge to ravish her.

She rolled over on her stomach then got up to her hands and knees. She lowered her upper body to the mattress. "Take me like this, my male."

"Rrrrssss." Alistair grabbed her hips and positioned himself behind her.

"Mmm, my male." She rubbed her ass against his hard cock.

He grabbed the head of his cock and positioned it at her opening then rammed his cock deeply into her. He leaned over her body as he continued to thrust his cock harder and harder.

"Oh Alistair," she moaned.

He leaned further over and bit her shoulder keeping her pinned under him.

"Yessss," she hissed as she enjoyed his grunts and growls while he thrust faster and harder. "Yes, yessss." Her orgasm ripped through her body with such a force she thought she might die from the pleasure of it.

"My female!!" he cried out as his body arched up, he continued to drive himself into her, slowly he thrust as his seed spurted out. He pulled his cock from her and let the remainder of his seed splash across her ass. "My female," he whispered as he watched his cum trickle down her ass.

"That was so good," she cooed as she stretched her body out. She gasped when he flipped her over and straddled her chest. He rubbed his cock across her breasts as it started to grow hard again.

"I need more of you," he groaned.

She reached up and grabbed his ass, pulling him closer. Her tongue teased the head of his cock. She looked up and saw him watching every movement of her tongue. She loved this feeling of power she had at this moment, loved the look of pleasure etched on his face. She gently suckled on the head of his cock as her hands kneaded his firm ass. He reached down and tangled his hands in her hair, lifting her head up closer to him.

"This feels so good," he said breathily. "So good."

She took more and more of his cock into her mouth. She purred when she felt him slowly begin to thrust and his hands tightening in her hair. She let his cock popped from her mouth briefly. "You taste so good, my male."

"Ahhhooo." He grabbed her head more firmly and eased his cock back into her mouth. "I am going to spill my seed…"

Anne slowed her sucking—she didn't want him to come yet. She took his cock from her mouth then lathed his cock with her tongue all the while watching his face. "You are so beautiful, Alistair," she purred.

"I need to come…Anne…ohhsssmm…"

"Grab your beautiful cock and stroke it for me. I want to taste your cum."

Alistair immediately did what she asked. He stroked his cock as she opened her mouth in anticipation of tasting his cum. He stroked faster and faster until his cum spurted from his cock into her mouth. She drank down every drop then licked the head of his cock.

Alistair climbed off her and laid on the bed beside her. "Say it again," he whispered as he pulled her into his arms.

"Say what again?"

"Tell me I am your male."

"You are my male, Alistair." She snuggled up against him. "My beautiful male."

Alistair kissed the top of her head and laid there just holding her closely to him. He never dreamed a female would willingly want him, or ever call him her male. His mind desperately scanned the conversation he had with Niro and Demos, he tried to remember what they said to their females when they wanted her to know just how much they adored them.

"I am not sure these words are right..." he paused. "I love you, Anne." His heart pounded in his chest. Perhaps it was too much to expect that she would have any feelings for him. She did call him her male...he held his breath waiting to see how she would react to his words of love.

Anne looked up into Alistair's pale blue eyes. "I love you too, Alistair." Her heart about melted when she saw the tears form in his eyes.

"Am I dreaming...am I dead?"

"What?" she propped herself up on her elbow.

"You love me, is this really true?"

"Yes, Alistair."

"You are a gift from our God. I never dreamt I would ever hear those words of love from a female."

"Oh Alistair." Her heart burst with love for him, but also ached knowing that he has never had someone say those words to him before.

"I swear I will make you happy and that I will protect you with my life," he said softly as he caressed her hair and gazed into her beautiful face.

෨෨෨෨

"Niro will be leaving tomorrow," Alistair said as he walked with Anne around the village.

"Does that mean Nina and Demos will be leaving too?"

"No, Demos is staying to command Niro's warriors that will be staying here for a little while. And where Demos is Nina will be."

"Do you honestly believe Nina is a good warrior? I think she is brave for wanting to be the first female warrior."

"Demos trained her, she must be a good warrior, though it is hard to see a female as a warrior. I was taught since I was very young that females are precious that they need a male's protection. So when I saw Nina for the first time it did throw me off balance. I have sparred with her and she is rather good, but still no match for a warrior of my caliber. She still has much to learn."

"But she is good right?"

"Oh yes, but the fact is a male is so much stronger than a female. Demos has taught her when to evade and when to strike. I believe she will be a grand warrior in time."

"You are a grand warrior."

"I have trained many years to get to this level."

"Oh...I see, so you are saying that after a few more years of training Nina will be just as good as the rest of the warriors."

"Yes."

"I have been hearing what a lot of these male warriors think about her."

"She doesn't care what they say. That is one of the things I really like about her. Besides if you notice most of these warriors won't say anything directly to her."

"They are afraid she might beat them in a match."

"No, they are afraid of Demos. He is a warrior of exceptional caliber. Not even I can beat him in a sparring match. I believe he can even beat Niro too."

"It sounds like you have great respect for Demos."

"Oh yes. I think all Dascon warriors respect him."

"Umm…can I ask something?"

"You can ask me anything, Anne."

"Why aren't you in charge of Niro's warriors?"

"I have to focus on getting the Larmat people ready to merge with the Dascon clan. If I command the Dascon warriors Niro brought with him this might bring fear to the Larmat people. I don't want this, Niro doesn't want this. We only want peace."

"I think I understand. I just thought maybe Niro was dissing you or something."

"Dissing?"

"Disrespecting you. If he was I was going to have a few words with him."

"Niro has great respect for me. You needn't worry about that, though I am touched that you are willing to challenge the leader of the Dascon clan for my honor." Alistair chuckled.

"Well…nobody better say anything bad about you in front of me or I will have to become the second female warrior on this planet."

Alistair's laughter warmed her.

"Tomar wants to start your training today."

"Really? This is so exciting."

"I will escort you to his chamber. You will be safe with the Rundals. Don't wander away from them."

"I won't. What are you going to do today?"

"I have to meet with Niro and Demos. Later on today I would like to spend time with little Zenos. Would you like to join me?"

"That would be wonderful."

Chapter Eight

Anne walked with the two Rundal guards to the conja's stable. She couldn't take her eyes off the reptilian males. Their body form was so much like a human males, she wondered if there was some human in their genes.

"Tomar is in the stable with one of the conjas," one of the males said.

Once inside the stable they led her to where Tomar was. He was examining a female conja.

"Hello Anne," Tomar said as he gently pet the conja.

"She is going to give birth isn't she?" Anne said. She went over to Tomar.

"Yes, any moment now. She is having a bit of trouble pushing the baby out."

Anne went to the other side. She petted the female conja's leg. "It's alright girl." She watched Tomar place his hands inside the conja and gently turned the baby. "It's alright," Anne said again, trying to calm the conja. Within moments a tiny baby conja emerged from its mother. "Oh...congratulations girl."

Tomar released the baby and reached for Anne. "We must leave them be now."

Anne went with Tomar to the other side of the pen. She watched the mother conja start to clean her infant. The little infant was so cute. "I would have thought a conja laid eggs."

"Only the birds and my people lay eggs to have offspring on this planet."

"Your people...really?"

"You seem surprised."

"It's just that you look…well almost human I would assume your females would have live births."

"Almost human huh." Tomar chuckled.

"Look at your body form, other than the tail, scales, rubbery skin and your reptilian facial features, you otherwise have the form of a human male."

"I guess we do."

"Is your reproductive organs the same as a human male too? Oh…I'm sorry I shouldn't have asked that."

"Your curiosity is pleasing to me. I have seen the male and female barbarian's reproductive organs and yes my people are very similar."

"Really?" Anne quickly looked away from him. She wanted to see for herself but there was no way that it would be proper to ask him.

"Juanas come here," Tomar said to one of the guards. "We Rundals are not bashful when it comes to our bodies. Juanas please take off your clothing."

Anne watched the male Rundal take off his loincloth. "Oh my…" she said, gazing at his black rubbery looking cock. "You are remarkably similar to human males."

"Thank you Juanas you may put your clothing back on. Anne don't tell Alistair that Juanas stood before you unclothed. Alistair may hurt him. The barbarian males are very jealous and protective of their females. So you can understand why I ask this of you."

"Of course. Is it possible for your people and the barbarians to mate?"

"Yes, but it doesn't produce offspring."

"Have the barbarians try to…"

"Sometimes, only if a female wishes it. Some of our females have started to crave the barbarians' rather rough mating."

"The male Rundals don't mate with the barbarian females?"

"No, the only female barbarians the male Rundal have a chance to encounter are those of the Dascon clan. Since almost all females of breeding age have a protector I will not allow any of my males to touch a female for fear that the barbarian males will hurt them. I am afraid I can't sate your curiosity about mating with any of the Rundal males. Alistair would kill any male, be it barbarian or Rundal that touches you."

"Oh...I didn't want to mate with...I am sorry I guess I should stop asking such personal questions."

"You may ask anything you wish."

Anne followed Tomar around the village as they checked various domestic animals. She even watched as he tended to the sick barbarians. His medical knowledge was awe-inspiring.

"How did you find Earth? How did you know that the females would be compatible with the barbarians?" Anne asked as they stopped for something to eat.

"Our ships can scan for life forms. Unfortunately we only have three working ships left at the moment. Finding Earth wasn't that hard, your chemical makeup is similar to the barbarians so I was hoping once we travel to Earth that your people would be physically similar and to my delight you are. The only real problem is the barbarians are larger than most Earthlings and tend to produce large offspring. Robin had a hard time carrying Zenos, it took quite the toll on her body. Sabrina had the same trouble and so has Jamie. I fear they may only produce one offspring for their mates."

"What about Nina?"

"Nina...she has yet to become pregnant. This of course is causing much talk."

"Talk?"

"Behind Demos and Nina's back, some male barbarians talk."

"What do they say?"

"That Nina can't produce offspring because she doesn't act like a female or that Demos doesn't mount Nina enough to produce offspring. There are many more things but I would rather not repeat them all."

"Not everyone gets pregnant right away."

"All barbarian males are very fertile once they drink the sacred juice. But for whatever reason the Dascon females are much more fertile than the Larmat females. I still haven't figured out why yet. Of course I haven't studied a Larmat female all that much yet."

"Poor Nina and Demos."

"They don't care what others say about them. This I admire."

"So, the Earth women won't be able to produce more than one baby."

"I fear that may be the case."

"Does Niro know this?"

"Yes, but I have found another planet where the people are very similar to the barbarians. The planet Loma. I have sent one of my ships over to scout it out."

"Another planet with life...wow. Of course I am still amazed just being on this planet."

"I have told Niro about my discovery. We both are eagerly awaiting the scouts' report."

"So does this mean no more females will be taken from Earth?"

"No, Niro wants to still bring females from Earth. We know your people are able to reproduce with the barbarians. I am not sure about the females on Loma yet."

"This is so mind blowing yet cool at the same time. Can you imagine the animal life on Loma. I wonder if they are similar to the animals on Earth or on Malka."

Tomar smiled. "I am very much enjoying our afternoon together. Once you are joined with Alistair I will begin your formal training."

"Joined?"

"I will let Alistair explained that to you. Speaking of Alistair I must bring you back to him. He mentioned that he would be with Robin and Zenos I shall have my guards take you there."

"Thank you Tomar this was a most delightful afternoon."

"Oh it was my pleasure."

Anne followed the two male Rundals back to the leader hut. They escorted her to Robin and Niro's chamber. When she walked in she saw Alistair playing peek-a-boo with little Zenos.

"Hello Anne." Robin walked over to her. "Zenos just loves when Alistair visits."

"I can see that."

"Anne." Alistair smiled at her. "Did you enjoy your time with Tomar?"

"Yes I did." She walked over to him. She sat down next to him.

"Boo, boo," Zenos said, stomping his little feet.

Alistair started playing peek-a-boo with him again. Anne couldn't help but smile at Zenos' infectious laughter. She looked up and saw Niro watching Alistair and Zenos playing. Strangely she felt at home here. The kind of home she remembered when her parents were alive…warmth, laughter…that safe and loved feeling. She wrapped her arms around one of Alistair's large arms and leaned her head against it. She watched Zenos take such delight in his game with Alistair.

Robin looked over at Niro and smiled. She was so happy that Alistair had found his mate. Just watching him and Anne anyone could see they belong together. Niro got up and walked over to Robin, he wrapped one of his arms around her.

"Are you alright little one?" he said.

"Yes…look at them," she whispered as she gestured subtly toward Anne and Alistair.

Niro kissed the top of her head. He too was happy that Alistair found a mate. Alistair deserved to find some happiness.

ಞಞಞ

Ivor waited outside the main Larmat village for Mace to report back to him. There was no way Ivor was going back to Rodan without Alistair's mate. The thought of his brother being disappointed with him he couldn't bear, not to mention his warrior's pride would be terribly wounded. He was angry at himself for letting his lust for Alistair's mate ruin the plan. When he saw her there alone…he had to have that woman. Now he is paying for his impulse. He perked up when he saw Mace headed toward him.

"What news do you have?" Ivor asked.

"Niro is leaving tomorrow. He will be taking half of his warriors back with him."

"Only half?"

"Demos will command the other half." Mace looked around. "Niro is looking for Rodan."

"How do you know this?"

"I heard talk about Niro's warriors searching each Larmat town looking for the rebel warriors. What if they have capture Rodan and the others?"

"My brother is no fool. He would have gone to the mountains."

"Ivor you must go back to your brother and tell him you failed. Rodan will come up with another plan."

"I won't tell him I failed. I will get Alistair's mate."

"How?"

"You will tell me where she is, when she might be alone."

"You can't go back into the village. Demos has told the guards about you. Besides, Alistair likes playing the part of a Dascon warrior—he will not leave his mate alone."

"He did for a moment before."

"After what you did he won't be leaving her alone again. You must tell Rodan you failed."

"I won't and I will kill any warrior who tells him about this. Now get back to the village. I will be camping here. Come and inform me of Alistair's movements. If I haven't capture Alistair's mate within the week I will go to Rodan." Ivor couldn't let his pride get in the way. Besides even if he had to sneak back into the village and risk death to capture the female he would do just that.

"Alright. With Niro gone Alistair might start his journeying from one village to another again."

"This would be perfect. Why do you have such a strange look to your face?"

"I was thinking...never mind."

"Out with it."

"Would it be so bad to let the clans join as one?"

"You are joking right. Of course it would be. Niro only wants all of Malka to be like Dascon, he cares little about our traditions."

"I ..." Mace looked nervous. "You will think me a traitor. Promise you will keep your sword sheath. I would never betray Rodan or you, but..."

"But what?"

"I stood guard beside a Dascon warrior while Niro and Alistair talked. All I heard Niro speak of was learning about our people. If he was going to take away our traditions why would he bother to learn about our people?"

"You are easily fooled. You stood guard because Niro wanted you to hear that, so you would help spread his lies."

"I am Alistair's guard…I have been since Alistair assumed leadership of our people."

"Then you should have killed him. Don't let Niro's lies or Alistair's compassion brain wash you."

"You are right. I am sorry."

"I am depending on you Mace. Prove to me you are still a Larmat warrior."

"I won't let you down Ivor."

Ivor watched Mace leave. This is not the first time Mace has had doubts. How could Mace believe Niro's lies? Niro only wants the Larmat females, the fertile lands of the Larmat villages. When he has obtained all of that he will start to kill the Larmat warriors. What Rodan has been saying is the truth. Ivor will get Alistair's female. Alistair would come to find her then Rodan will kill Alistair. Rodan will be named the ruler of the Larmat people. Ivor settled into his campsite. He would give Mace three days, if Mace hasn't returned with news Ivor was going to sneak back inside the village take Alistair's mate and if necessary he would kill Mace as well.

Chapter Nine

Alistair had a firm grip on Anne's head as she sucked at his cock. He awoke to this wonderful pleasure. He spread his legs further apart as she slowly bobbed her head on his cock. He didn't want this bliss to end, damn her mouth felt so good on his cock.

"My female…my sweet female," he purred. He looked down and watched half of his cock disappear in her mouth. He had to close his eyes or he was in danger of coming right now. The soft sucking sounds she made was driving him crazy, her sweet moans vibrated on his cock making it that more difficult for him to hold back from coming. He heard his cock pop from her mouth. He looked down quickly when he felt her wet tongue begin to lick at his balls as her hand slowly stroked his cock. He could feel her start to gently suck on his balls as her hand stroked his cock faster and faster.

"I am going to come…oh I am going to come."

"Oh no you're not…not yet anyways."

Anne moved her hand down to the base of his cock and gripped it firmly. She waited for his breathing to calm down before she started licking the head of his cock.

Alistair watched her face as she took much delight in tasting him. He tightened his grip on her head. "Stop teasing me," he growled. That mischievous grin that swept across her face drove him crazy. He pushed down on her head wanting her to take his cock back in her mouth. "Please," he whispered. She opened her mouth and allowed him to guide her head. His hips thrust upwards wanting to bury his cock in her throat. It took every ounce of his willpower not to just ram his cock down her throat. "Take more, oh please take all of my cock into your beautiful mouth." He lifted his upper body up so he could watch her swallow his cock. When she had every last inch of him down her throat he fell back into the bed. "OHHHMMM," he moaned loudly. He grabbed handfuls of her hair and helped her to bob her head on his cock. With each down stroke she swallowed all of his cock. "My female...oh I am going to come. I can't stop it." His upper body arched up as his amazing orgasm rocked his body. His cum sprayed down her throat and she greedily drank every last drop of it. He released her head and just laid there as she gently licked the head of his cock.

"That was yummy," she said as she kissed the head of his cock.

"Come here female, sit on my face. I want to lick your pussy until you scream." He reached down and lifted her up. "Now female." He slapped her ass hard as he positioned her over his face. He gripped her ass firmly as he licked hungrily at her pussy.

"Damn...oh damn," she moaned as his tongue lapped at her. The eagerness of his tongue quickly brought her to orgasm. "Yessss," she hissed when he stuck his tongue deep inside her. He grabbed her ass hard and began moving her hips back and forth, rubbing her pussy all over his face.

"Alistair, I am going to come again." She reached down and grabbed his hair as she rubbed her pussy faster and faster against his face. This second orgasm was stronger than the first. She felt his tongue lap up her sweet nectar. She started to climb off of him, but he slapped her ass hard and held her in place.

"Sit down on my face, female. I want to eat you until you scream my name." He took her clit into his mouth and gently sucked.

The mixture of sensations he was causing between the sucking, licking and rubbing was driving her mad. She had several smaller orgasms. "Alistair…" she moaned loudly as he buried his tongue deeply into her, then he darted his tongue in and out of her. She couldn't stop herself from moving her hips up and down she wanted to fuck his tongue. "Alistair…" Her breathing quickened. His tongue moved in and out and flicked back and forth, he alternated this movement over and over. Her head arched back as her orgasm began to build. She tightened her hold on his hair as he slapped her ass with each thrust of his tongue. She held her breath as her orgasm reached its pinnacle. "Alistair!!!" she screamed out. She felt his growls vibrate over her pussy. He flipped her over to her back

"Rrrrr…female," he growled as he positioned himself between her legs.

"Fuck me…now Alistair take me…fuck me hard."

He gripped her hips then drove his cock into her. He thrust hard and fast burying his cock deeply into her with each stroke.

His growls were driving her crazy. "Harder, harder. Harder!!" she cried out.

"AHHHRRRRHHH!" he cried out as he drove his cock so hard and fast into her, he hoped he wasn't going to hurt her.

"Come Alistair, come now!" she moaned as she rode the wave of her orgasm.

Alistair thrust faster and faster until he came. He collapsed down onto her. He felt her arms and legs wrap tightly around him. He lifted himself up on his elbows and looked down into her face. "That was a wonderful way to wake up." He smiled at her.

"Yeah it was."

She released her hold on him and he rolled off of her. She snuggled up against him.

"Niro has left already. He wanted to get an early start."

"I wish I had a chance to say goodbye to Robin."

"Don't worry we will visit the Dascon village once everything is settled here."

"Alistair…you do know I have to return to Earth at the end of the six months. I have to find my parents' murderers."

"I know. I would never stop you from doing what you felt you needed to do." Alistair slowly sat up. He moved to the side of the bed and placed his feet on the floor.

"You have no idea how much that means to me. I was afraid you might try and stop me." She moved over to him and snuggled against his back.

"Finding the ones responsible for your parent's death is very important to you. You need this and I am here to give you what you need. But…allow me to join you."

"I don't know Alistair. My planet is so much different than yours."

"I need to be with you, no matter where that is."

"But your people need you here."

"I need you Anne, allow me to join you on your planet."

Anne hugged him tighter and laid her head against his strong back. "You will find it hard to adjust to my planet."

"In other words I won't fit in. I don't fit in on my own world and yet I adapt."

She could tell by the tone of his soft, deep voice how important this was to him. She couldn't deny him. "Alright Alistair you can come with me. That's if Niro will allow you to leave."

"Niro won't be able to keep me away from you."

Anne kissed his back then climbed out of bed. She wrapped her covering around herself. She spotted the book Niro gave to Alistair earlier sitting on the table next to the bed. "Did you read the book Niro gave you?"

"Not yet." Alistair reached down and grabbed his loincloth. He stood up and put it on.

"Why not?"

"I don't have time right now."

"It's about your father, aren't you curious what it is written about him in there?"

"If you like you may read it. You should know about where I came from."

"That wouldn't be right, you should read it first."

Alistair grabbed the book and handed it to Anne. "I want you to read it. I have to talk with Demos and plan out where to go from here with getting the Larmat people to accept the joining of the clans."

"I don't understand if I could find something out about my father that I didn't know I would have read that book right away."

"Your father was with you. I barely remember my father. If he loved me and my mother so much why didn't he take us away? Why bring us back to a Dascon village then leave? Your mother and father lived together in love. My mother had to live in loneliness waiting for my father to come to her, all because they were from two different clans."

"My parents were from two different races."

"And yet your father endured whatever was thrown at him to be with your mother. Mine didn't."

"Your father wanted to keep you safe. Please Alistair read the book about your father in the Larmat history vault, read this book."

"Anne I must go talk with Demos."

"Alistair stop running away. Demos can wait. I read that book in the Larmat vault. Your father loved you."

"Anne!" Alistair barked, causing her to back away from him a little. "I am sorry, please don't fear me. I just can't think about my father now, please understand this. I want you to read that book for I can't right now."

"Alright. I am sorry for pushing you so hard."

"I will post a guard by the door. If you wish to journey around the village please allow the guard to escort you."

Anne nodded her head yes. Alistair pulled her to him and kissed her deeply then he left the room. Anne slowly sat down on the bed. She gently caressed the cover to the book that was simply titled "For Alistair". She sat back into the bed and opened the book.

Alistair,

I know you probably don't remember me and what memories you have are vague. But I want you to know I loved your mother with all my heart. I didn't care what clan she belonged to. And I loved you beyond words to describe, my son. I have told Hakan my story and I hope he keeps his word and passes it on to you. Maybe then you will understand why I couldn't take you and your mother off to the mountains. I am sorry my son for the cruelties you will suffer because your parents were from two different clans. You were born out of love. You are not an abomination, you are our beloved son. If only my sword was swifter and my arms stronger I could have killed all those who will harm you with there hurtful words. The only thing I can give you, my son, is your life which I gladly trade mine to make sure that you can live that life.

The sword your mother will give you when you have grown into a strong warrior is mine. I pray that you wield it better than I have. Hakan has agreed to train you and he will keep you and your mother safe. He is a good man. You will be confused why I chose to go to the leader of my people's enemy. Your mother opened my eyes. She told me about Hakan and his compassion. My people won't accept you, Alistair. For this I am ashamed. I only pray that Hakan will make his people accept you.

Written in this book is my life. I wanted so much to tell you these tales myself when you were old enough to understand, but your safety is the most important thing to me. I pray that you think well of me. More importantly I hope you will give your mother some peace. Leaving her, leaving you is my greatest sorrow.

I love you Alistair more than any father could love his son. I am proud to call you my son. I pray that you will one day be proud to call me your father. One day you will announce to your offspring that you are the son of Tibor.

Anne wiped away her tears as she closed the book. Memories flooded her. Her father's own struggle to keep her safe from prejudice, Alistair's father wanted the same thing. Things were tough on her when she was growing up, but she couldn't even begin to imagine what it must have been like for Alistair. Only a handful of people on this planet accepted him. At least for her she only had to deal with a few narrow-minded idiots. Still, the results were the same, Alistair lost his father and she lost her parents to hatred.

"Why?!" she cried out. The familiar emptiness, anger and sorrow racked her mind. Now her empathy for Alistair magnified these feelings. Here on Malka everyone didn't see her as different, they easily accepted her. But Alistair would never be accepted. She would have to see the looks, hear the whispers about him. It would break her heart.

"I need to be with you, no matter where that is." His words filled her mind. On Earth he could live without

those looks or whispers. But...his people needed him though they can't accept him. Niro must have great confidence in Alistair's abilities. And so it goes around and around in her head until she wanted to scream. She hugged her pillow tightly and allowed herself to cry as images of her parents flashed in her mind. "Alistair," she whispered, wishing she had his strong arms around her now. She couldn't keep him from doing his important work. Then fear slowly started to creep in. How could she need him so much this fast? He has her heart—he took it without her knowing he did. Now he was threatening to take her soul. His beautiful pale blue eyes filled with so much life, love and pain flashed in her mind.

"I love you," his soft deep voice echoed in her head.

This was all almost too much, maybe she was dreaming. The one thing she did know is that she couldn't leave him, not now...not ever. This thought scared her most of all.

Chapter Ten

Anne finished getting ready. Alistair did say it was okay for her to wander around the village as long as she took her guard with her. She had no desire to stay in this room. She read the entire book Hakan made for Alistair. Tibor was a good man and a grand warrior. He loved Alistair's mother very much. Anne tried not to think about that book. Alistair should read it, he had to read it.

She opened the door startling the large blond-haired warrior who stood guard in front of it.

"You shouldn't leave your room."

"Alistair said I could walk around the village as long as you came with me."

"I think he was referring to the Dascon warrior that was here. I am giving him a break."

"You will do just fine. What is your name?"

"I am called Mace."

"Please call me Anne."

"I can only address you as Alistair's mate."

Anne thought that was so silly, but didn't argue with her escort. She headed out of the leader hut, Mace was right behind her.

Mace watched Anne as she wandered through the market area. This was his chance to help Ivor capture her. He found himself wrestling with his conscience. Alistair treated him no different than he treated the Dascon warriors. Just the fact that Alistair allowed several Larmat warriors to stay in the village and continue to train and do their duties said a lot to Mace. He could hear Niro's words rattling around in his mind. Niro never spoke ill of the

Larmat people. He honestly seemed to want to understand their culture. Rodan's words were always filled with venom, but Niro...

"Mace what is going on?" Anne pointed to two large Larmat warriors circling each other with their swords drawn.

"They both want the same female."

"Shouldn't you stop them?"

"Why? The victor will take the female. This is how it has always been done."

Anne could see the beautiful blonde female the two warriors were fighting over. Her clothes were ripped and she looked afraid. No one came to her aid; in fact they kept their distance from her.

"She doesn't want to be with either of them," Anne said as she tried to move closer to the frighten woman.

"What she wants doesn't matter. Now stay here." Mace grabbed Anne's arm.

"This is bullshit. Alistair wouldn't allow this."

"Alistair isn't here. He can't change the way us Larmat have lived."

Anne watched as one of the warriors pinned the other under him. After the one conceded defeat the victor went over to the frightened woman and threw her over his shoulder.

Anne looked away. She couldn't believe no one was going to help that poor woman. The crowd started to walk away. Anne was startled when she felt Mace lift her up. He held her to him with one arm and used his other hand to cover her mouth. Anne started to panic. Was he planning on raping her? She knew this was a real possibility given Mace was a Larmat warrior.

Mace moved with speed he didn't know he possessed as he carried her out of the village. He only prayed no one spotted him. A part of him didn't want to do this, but he had to remain loyal to Rodan and to his people.

"I am sorry," he whispered as he darted into the forest still holding her close to him. He could feel her squirm trying to free herself.

"Ivor!" he cried out.

Anne's eyes widened when she saw Ivor emerge from the trees.

"Mace..." Ivor was thrilled to see Alistair's mate in Mace's arms. "I was beginning to doubt your loyalty to Rodan."

"Here take her." Mace set Anne down then pushed her toward Ivor. "I don't want to see what you will do to her. I must head back." Mace was surprised when Ivor's sword went threw his leg. "What?"

"We have to make it look like you were attacked. Otherwise Alistair will kill you." Ivor pulled his sword from Mace's leg. "Now go. Tell Alistair I took his mate."

Anne tried to free herself from Ivor's grasp as she watched Mace limp away. "Let me go!" She punched at his arm.

Ivor threw her over his shoulder and headed back into the forest. He walked for about a mile. Anne could hear the familiar sound of a conja flapping its wings. She pounded on Ivor's back but it was futile. He climbed on the back of the conja then placed her in front of him. He held her to him with one arm and grabbed the reins with the other.

"You feel my hard cock pressing against you female?" Ivor pulled her closer to him. "When I get enough distance between me and Alistair I am going to bury my cock deeply in you, first your pussy then your mouth."

"You are not going to touch me."

Ivor started to laugh as his conja took to the sky.

Anne closed her eyes and tried to center herself. She had to think of a way to get away from him. She remembered reading about how the Larmat people thought it was crazy how a Dascon male risk everything to save his female. Many Dascon males had attack the main Larmat village by themselves trying to rescue their mate and all but Niro had failed. Niro would have too if it wasn't for Robin escaping the village herself and Demos showing up just when he did. This is what these assholes wanted—they wanted Alistair to come by himself to rescue her. She wouldn't allow this to happen. Alistair would be killed.

She opened her eyes when she felt the conja start to descend. She quickly looked around, she couldn't see the Larmat village anymore. They must have flown for hours. She felt the bump when the conja landed and Ivor dismounted. She tried to quickly get off the conja on the other side but Ivor grabbed her before she could.

"You can't escape me." He tore her covering from her body.

"Don't touch me."

Ivor removed his loincloth and lunged at her. She kicked as hard as she could hitting him in the balls. He fell to the ground. She quickly started running into the forest. She didn't care she was naked. Her only thought was getting away from him. She ran and ran as fast and as far as she could. She stopped briefly—all she could see was forest. She had no idea where she was or even which way to run.

"Arrrhhh!" Ivor growled angrily.

She felt a strong pair of hands on her shoulders, then the next thing she knew she was laying face down on the ground.

"I am going to fuck you until you bleed for kicking me like that. Did you honestly believe you could escape me?"

She was powerless to stop what he was going to do to her. She felt his cock enter her as he started to thrust violently into her.

He used her body for hours until she was too sore to move.

He dragged her back to where his conja was and put his loincloth back on. He tossed what remain of her covering to her. "You are my female now, pretty one."

"I am Alistair's female."

"Rodan will kill Alistair so you might as well start mourning his death. But make no mistake you are mine now. You will bear me many strong sons."

"You hurt Alistair and I will kill you."

"Rodan, my brother, will hurt Alistair. Then I will chop off Alistair's head and send it back to Niro."

"I won't allow anyone to hurt Alistair."

"What can you really do about it female? Mmm, that fire in your eyes is making my cock hard again."

"Don't you touch me again you filthy animal. When Alistair and his warriors do show up they will kill you all."

"Alistair will not bring any warriors. He will come alone, like any other Dascon fool."

"You will be dead by then anyways." Anne glared at him.

"Really? This is most entertaining. You kill me." Ivor started to laugh as he walked over to her. He pulled her over to him. "I must get you back to my brother or otherwise I would take you again." He grabbed a handful of her hair and forced her to look him in the eye. "Listen female, your only purpose is to bear offspring and bring pleasure to the strongest of males. If you please me I will protect you from other males, if you don't I will simply throw you to them. The sooner you accept this the better you will be. I am a strong warrior and very able to protect you. Alistair is going to die, so you may want to try and get on my good side. Otherwise that sweet pussy of yours will bring pleasure to many warriors. Larmat males are nothing like those pathetic Dascon males. Remember that the next time you try to deny me anything."

He let her down and climbed onto the conja. He pulled her over to him and pulled her up placing her in front of him. "I will have new coverings brought for you. It wouldn't do to have you running around half naked in front of the other warriors. I don't feel like fighting off all of them." He kicked the sides of the conja and it took flight.

Anne didn't know how she was going to help Alistair. Would he come alone or would he bring his warriors with him?

ΩΩΩ

Alistair quickly entered his chamber when he saw no guard at the door. "Anne," he called out, and was greeted only with silence. He went to the bathing chamber then to the balcony. His heart started to pound in his chest. Where was she? He quickly calmed down when he remembered that he did tell her she could look around the village. That would explain why the guard wasn't at his post.

"Alistair," a deep male voice said.

Alistair looked up and saw the Dascon warrior who was suppose to be guarding Anne.

"Where is my female?"

"Mace stood guard. You instructed it was okay if we switch on and off guard duty."

"When was this?"

"Hours ago. Do you want me to search the village for them?"

"Yes." Alistair followed the warrior out of the leader hut and started looking through the village himself.

"Alistair!" Nina cried out.

He quickly hurried over to her. He didn't like that look on her face.

"You must come with me," Nina said as she took off toward the leader hut.

Alistair's heart about stopped when he saw Demos tending to Mace's wounded leg.

"Where is my female?" Alistair growled.

"I was attacked just outside the village by Ivor. He took your female."

"Why did you leave the village?"

"Your female wanted to look around. I thought it would be okay if we stayed close to the village. I am sorry Alistair."

"It isn't your fault."

"How do you know this Larmat warrior didn't take your female to Ivor?" Demos said as he stood and glared at Mace.

"He is my guard. I don't doubt what he is saying."

"You are too trusting Alistair."

"Ivor wants you to know where he took her. He said to tell you to meet him in the village of Exoida. This is the only reason he let me live."

Alistair squatted down and looked at the large wrappings around Mace's leg. "Are you injured badly?"

"No…nothing a little time would heal."

"Why didn't Ivor wound you badly? He only needed you to stay alive long enough to deliver his message," Demos said still glaring at Mace.

"Because I am a Larmat warrior, if I was a Dascon warrior he would have done just that."

"Yeah a Larmat warrior he would perceive as a traitor."

"Demos enough," Alistair said. "Take Mace to my hut and send for a healer. Help him Nina."

"Don't leave until we have secured enough warriors to attack Exoida," Demos said as he helped Mace to his feet. "Did you hear me Alistair?"

"I heard you."

He waited for Demos and Nina to go into the leader hut, then he rushed to the stables. He saddled up his conja and then took flight.

Nina helped Mace to lie down. "Demos…" She looked over to him. "You know Alistair has already left."

"I know, so we must work quickly."

"I will send for a healer stay right there," she said to Mace. She led Demos from the room. "With Alistair gone someone has to stay and look over this village. Once those Larmat warriors get word that Alistair has left they might start to fight."

"Damn Larmat." Demos knew she was right. Alistair always appointed a temporary leader of the village before he left.

"You have to stay Demos. I will go help Alistair."

"NO!" Demos bellowed. "He is walking into an ambush. There will be many warriors there. I will not allow you to go alone. I can't…" Demos pulled her into his arms. "Please Nina…I will send several Dascon warriors to aid Alistair but I can't risk you."

"But you have trained me. I can help Alistair."

"Please Nina for me don't go. I will have no choice but to follow you."

"Alright Demos I will stay with you. But you must send your warriors right now."

Demos kissed her softly then hurried off to round up at least ten of his finest warriors who were in this village.

Nina walked back into the room where Mace had been and was surprised that he wasn't there. "What the hell?" She hurried through the leader hut and couldn't find

Mace anywhere. He was wounded where could he have gone. She walked out of the leader hut and saw a conja leave the stables. She could only make out that the rider had long golden hair. She hurried over to where the warrior huts were. She spotted Demos gathering up some warriors.

"Demos!" she cried out.

He hurried over to her. "What is it?"

"Mace is gone. I am pretty sure that was him who just flew his conja out of here."

"I knew that bastard was part of this. We must hurry." Demos knew it would take him at least a half hour to get all the warriors needed then decide who was going to lead them. He could only hope they reached Alistair in time. He instructed his warriors to bring Mace back alive if they could. He wanted to kill Mace himself. How could Mace betray Alistair like that, especially after what Alistair had done for him.

Chapter Eleven

Anne was exhausted when they reached Exoida. Ivor landed his conja and then jumped off of it. He pulled Anne off and held her in his arms.

"Ivor!"

"Rodan!" Ivor set Anne down as Rodan approached.

Anne looked over at the large blond-haired warrior, he looked identical to Ivor.

"This is Alistair's mate?" Rodan asked, letting his eyes linger over Anne's body.

"Once you kill Alistair this female will be mine," Ivor said.

"Until then however…" Rodan moved closer to Anne. Her half-naked body was exciting him. He reached his hand out and she coiled back. "I won't hurt you female." He moved his hand tenderly down her arm. He liked the bronze of her skin, the silky feel of it against his calloused hands. "Alistair doesn't deserve this female. What clan is she from? Her dark hair…she must be Dascon, but yet her bronze skin is neither Larmat nor Dascon."

"She is from the new planet the Rundals found for those Dascon scum."

"Once we regain our lands back and kill Niro and his offspring we will force the Rundals to bring us many females from this planet. Those Dascon warriors who have women from this planet…Saa and his fire-haired female, Demos and his warrior female, Niro and Samson's females are so small and delicate. And now this bronze beauty, there had to be other females brought to Malka with her, too."

"I heard Leo and Ezra have become those new ones protectors."

"And yet the great Niro doesn't allow Larmat warriors to possess such rare females. Ivor let me sample this female."

"Once…but when she is my female I won't allow any other male to touch her."

"Agreed."

Anne fought hard to break Rodan's hold on her, but he dragged her to one of the huts.

"Be quick Rodan. Alistair will no doubt be here soon." Ivor headed off to find Anne some new coverings.

Rodan threw Anne onto the bed once they entered the hut. He quickly removed his loincloth. "Listen carefully female…if you willingly give your body to me I won't hurt you. But if you force me to take you against your will I will show no mercy."

Anne lay on the bed and opened her legs. She was startled when he flipped her over and entered her from behind. She closed her eyes and pictured Alistair…yes Alistair was the one taking her now. Rodan was true to his word and didn't hurt her. He left her lying there as he exited the hut. She could hear the footsteps of a warrior as he stood guard in front of the hut she was in.

Ivor headed over to the hut where Anne was being kept. He managed to find a new covering for her.

"Wait brother," Rodan said, grabbing Ivor's arm.

"Leave her as she is until after I have killed Alistair. Let that miserable half-breed see what we have done to his female."

"Alright…I guess." Ivor set the covering next to the hut.

"Warriors of the Larmat clan!" Rodan bellowed. "Ready yourself. Alistair will be here soon and no doubt that scum Demos will send warriors after him. I will kill that half-breed Alistair and we will kill any Dascon warrior who steps foot in this village."

Anne heard several warriors roar out their battle cries. There had to be at least twenty or more Larmat warriors out there. "Alistair…" Anne looked around for any way she could get out of this damn hut, but there was only one way in or out. There were no windows or anything in this small hut. How was she going to get pass the large warrior who guarded the entrance? If she could escape Alistair won't have to fight to save her. She got up and put on the tattered covering. She searched every inch of the hut, there was no escape.

She sat down on the dirt floor. "Damn it Alistair…please don't come here alone." She felt dirty after being used by Ivor and Rodan. She was so powerless to stop them and now she is powerless to help Alistair. Rage and despair boiled up in her. She couldn't let Alistair die, there had to be something she could do…she pulled her legs up to her chest and hugged them tightly. She couldn't stop what happened to her parents and now…Alistair. She started to quietly sing to herself.

Ivor leaned up against the door of the hut when he heard her beautiful voice. He couldn't understand what she was singing, but her voice was heavenly just like the elder females. The sooner Alistair died the quicker he could claim this female as his. He laid his head on the door and just listened to her sing.

ಐ ಐ ಐ

Alistair saw the village of Exioda coming over the horizon. He knew Ivor would have an ambush waiting from him, but he had to get Anne away from them. He couldn't even think about what those Larmat warriors had probably done to her, he couldn't allow himself. The rage would blind him. He had to stay focused—if he died she would be left to suffer an unimaginable fate. He drew his bow. He held onto the conja firmly with his legs and applying gentle pressure he directed the animal to descend. He pulled the bowstring back and took aim. Any Larmat warrior who lived in this village was a target.

Ivor ducked out of the way when the warrior who stood beside him fell to the ground with an arrow sticking out of his chest.

"Rodan, Alistair has come!" Ivor cried out. He drew his sword and took cover. Alistair would have to land sometime.

"Alistair!" Anne hurried to the door. She tried to open it but it was locked. "Damn it!" she cried, pounding the door.

Rodan stood in the middle of the village and drew his bow. He carefully aimed. "Ivor bring the female out now."

Ivor hurried over to the hut Anne was in and quickly opened the door. He grabbed Anne firmly by the arm and pulled her out.

Alistair saw Rodan though he believed it was Ivor he was targeting. He had the advantage being on the conja. He pulled his bowstring back further...he had to wait for the precise moment. He released the bow too early when he saw Ivor holding onto Anne. He was confused by the sight of Rodan and Ivor, they looked identical to one another. His eyes locked on Anne and the tattered covering she was wearing. Anger surged through him. He heard the conja let out an awful shrill noise, then it fell from the sky. Alistair and the conja hit the ground with a thud.

Alistair forced himself to his feet. He reached back and grabbed his sword. Luckily the conja took the brunt of the fall.

"Let my female go!" Alistair thundered.

"You will have to kill both of us first, half-breed," Ronar said, dropping his bow and reaching back for his sword.

"Alistair go, please leave there are too many of them!" Anne shouted out as she fought to free herself from Ivor's grasp.

"He won't go female, so save your words. Dascon males are weak when it comes to their females. Why do you risk your life for this pretty one, half-breed? I am sure Niro will find you another female. I would have let my enemy have her, she can be replaced."

"She is my life, I swore to protect and love her. You wouldn't know the honor or joy this brings a male, one female to love and protect forever—one female who gives me her love. What good does having many females do if none of them gives you her heart? A moment of pleasure pales to a lifetime of love."

"Shut up!" Rodan rushed at Alistair.

Anne could only watch as Alistair and Rodan fought. She had to do something, anything.

"Watch female, watch my brother slay that half-breed."

"Don't you dare call Alistair a half-breed." Anne kicked and bit at Ivor until he released her. She rushed over to where Rodan dropped his bow. She tried her best to pull the bowstring back, but she just didn't have the strength to do it. She saw Ivor slowly walking over to her with a smile on his face. She dropped the bow but held the arrow firmly in her hand.

"You are amusing me so much female." Ivor lifted his hand to the approaching warriors. "Save your strength warriors. You will need it when those Dascon warriors arrive."

"What if Demos comes with them?" one of the younger warriors said.

"Don't worry I will kill him." Ivor moved closer to Anne. "You are making me miss watching the fight between Rodan and Alistair. You run from me again and I will let all these warriors fuck you."

Anne looked over to Alistair. *Please defeat Rodan, oh God let Alistair win.* She prayed silently. She gripped the arrow tighter in her hand. She could feel the heat from Ivor's body as he stood right behind her. What was she going to do? She had to do something...anything.

Alistair fought with everything he had. He had to win and he had to do it quickly. There were at least twenty other Larmat warriors to fight. He knew in his mind there was no way he could fight them all. He would have to buy some time for Demos' warriors to show up. He glanced over quickly and saw Anne standing there in front of Ivor. She was safe for now. Ivor was too interested in the battle, but if Alistair won...he had to make Rodan get closer to Ivor.

"You filthy half-breed what made you think you were worthy to rule my people? What makes Niro think my people want to join with his clan? No...I won't let Niro destroy my clan and I sure the hell won't stand for a half-breed leading my people."

Alistair felt his sword vibrate. Rodan's rage was unstoppable. He wasn't expecting for Rodan to punch him and it sent him crashing to the ground.

"Alistair!!" Anne yelled. She moved with speed she didn't think she possessed. She just missed being grabbed by Ivor. She had to do something. Rodan lifted his sword up to strike Alistair as Alistair laid dazed for a moment on the ground.

Alistair looked up and watched Rodan grimace. Alistair struck like a cobra embedding his sword in Rodan's gut. Rodan fell to the ground and Alistair quickly got up to his feet. He saw the arrow in Rodan's back and Anne standing there.

"Alistair…"

He grabbed her quickly and placed her behind him.

"I want you to run into the forest," Alistair said as he rushed at Ivor.

"Kill her, kill that fucking bitch!!" Ivor yelled. His brother was dead…because of her.

"Anne!" Alistair pushed Ivor back and ran back to Anne. He blocked the sword of one of the warrior's but another sliced Alistair across the arm. "Run Anne, please run."

She quickly started to run to the forest but was stopped by Ivor. "You will watch Alistair die, then I will kill you slowly," he growled. He turned her around and pulled her hair forcing her to look toward Alistair.

Alistair was trying so hard to fight off the four warriors who were attacking him.

"Let me go," she said, struggling. She couldn't stand this. Alistair's skin being sliced, they were toying with him, making him suffer.

Two of the warriors fell to the ground with arrows in their chest. The other two charged at the Dascon warriors who entered the village. Ivor grimaced and pulled the arrow from his arm. He looked up and saw Nina on the conja.

"I will not let a female defeat me." He pushed Anne to the ground and placed his sword at her neck. "Get down here you bitch or she dies."

Nina landed her conja and pulled her sword from its sheath. Ivor laughed and raised his blade to embed it in Anne's neck. Anne closed her eyes and awaited death then quickly looked up when she heard a slicing sound, she saw blood pouring from Ivor's mouth.

"I believe Niro will bring peace to Malka," Mace said as he pushed Ivor to the ground. He fell to the ground, his leg unable to support his weight anymore. He threw his sword down and awaited Demos' punishment. A sadness swept over him as he watched Anne hurry over to Alistair's still body.

"You did this," Demos growled as he lifted his sword to behead Mace.

"No Demos." Nina grabbed Demos' arm. "He saved Anne."

"I accept my fate. Do with me what you will," Mace said.

"I will deal with you later." Demos couldn't kill Mace not with that look in Nina's eyes. He couldn't worry about it now. He rushed over to Alistair.

Anne tore the tattered remnants of her covering. She had to stop the bleeding. She quickly used all of her covering to stem Alistair's bleeding. She didn't care that she was naked in front of all these people. All that matter was Alistair.

Demos quickly tore the cloth opening to one of the smaller huts down and went to Anne. He covered her with the cloth. He looked down at Alistair's pale face. "We must get him back to the main village. Tomar is still there."

"You can't move him in this condition," Anne said. She felt Alistair's hand reach up and gently grab her hair.

"You are alright." He weakly smiled.

"And you will be too." She smiled back. She grabbed his hand and cradled it to her face.

"I will protect your female while you heal," Demos said.

"Demos...take Anne back to Earth...very important..."

"I will do as you ask."

"You are coming with me, Alistair." Anne kissed his hand.

"You have given me a moment of peace…thank you Anne."

"Don't you dare die on me. You promised to protect me and I am keeping you to that promise. Alistair…I love you."

Alistair passed out.

"Anne we have to get him to Tomar. It's his only chance," Nina said.

Anne got up and allowed Demos to carry Alistair to a conja. Demos climbed on behind Alistair. "I will hurry. Nina bring Anne back to the village."

"We better find you some clothes first."

"Thank you for coming to help Alistair."

"Demos was suppose to stay at the village, but his warriors wouldn't leave without him. Demos appointed a young warrior commander while we were gone. I am so glad we got here in time to save you. I only wish we could have…"

"Alistair will be alright!" Anne barked. "Don't act like he is going to die."

"I am sorry, Anne."

Anne walked over to the hut that used to hold her prisoner. She grabbed a covering that lay beside it. She quickly put it on.

"Let's go," Nina said.

"Wait." Anne hurried over and picked up Alistair's sword. "Alistair can't lose this."

"The blacksmith would have made him another one just like it."

"No, Alistair has to have this sword. It was his father's sword."

"Alistair never mentioned that before."

"I don't think he knows yet. Let's go."

Nina climbed onto her conja and helped Anne get on behind her. They took off and headed for the village.

When they arrived at the village Demos greeted them. "I was beginning to get worried. It is almost nightfall and the wild conjas…"

"I am okay. Susie isn't as fast as your conja."

"Where is Alistair?" Anne rushed over to them.

"Tomar is wrapping him in the healing bandages."

"Take me to him."

"Let Tomar heal Alistair."

"I have to…be with him." Anne started to cry.

"Shh," Demos said as Nina wrapped her arms around Anne. "Niro was far worse when I found him outside this village."

Anne looked up at Demos.

"Alistair is strong. Let Tomar's healing bandages have time to work. You need to rest. I promise Alistair I would protect you while he healed."

"But…"

"Alistair won't hear you in the wrap and Demos is right you need to rest."

Anne reluctantly followed Nina back to Alistair's chamber. "Where is Alistair?"

"He is in Tomar's chamber. Would you like me to stay with you tonight?"

"No, thank you. I am very tired."

"Get your rest. Tomorrow I will take you to Alistair."

Anne watched Nina leave the room. There was no way she was going to stay in here. She had to see Alistair. She was going to find Tomar's chamber. She waited a few moments then opened the door. A very large Dascon warrior was standing guard.

"Demos has instructed that you not leave your chamber."

"I am going to find Alistair. You can help me do this or I will wander around all by myself."

"You can't do that."

"Try to stop me." Anne started to walk away but the guard grabbed her.

"I will show you where Alistair is."

"Thank you," she said quietly.

The guard led her to Tomar's chamber. He knocked on the door then stepped aside. "I will stand guard. If you wish to go back to your chamber I will escort you."

"Anne, please come in. I somehow knew you wouldn't listen to Demos."

"Can I please see Alistair?"

"Of course, but he is wrapped in the healing bandages." Tomar gently touched her shoulder. "Don't worry Alistair will be alright. He only needs time to heal. Luckily your efforts saved him from losing too much blood."

He led her to a small room. Anne saw a man wrapped completely in bandages reminding her of a mummy. She looked up at Tomar.

"That is Alistair. I will give you some privacy."

She walked over and sat down next to him. "Alistair," she whispered. She placed her hand gently on his bandaged chest. She closed her eyes and tried to remember the words of that Larmat lullaby, but she could only remember the melody. She began to softly hum the melody. She sang several songs to him everything she could think of that had a gentle rhythm, she sang and sang until she fell asleep beside him.

Chapter Twelve

Anne stayed by Alistair's side for three days while he lay wrapped in the bandages. Every night she would sing to him, hoping he could hear her, then she would fall asleep sitting on a chair beside his bed.

The next morning Alistair broke free of the bandages. He could see the soft light began to fill the room as the suns slowly rose in the morning sky. He looked over his body and to his amazement all his wounds were healed. The Rundal were truly remarkable beings. He looked over to the side of the bed and saw Anne. She was sitting on a chair with her upper body lying on the side of the bed. He could still hear her beautiful voice in his head—still remember the songs she sang to him. Though his body was still weak he leaned over and gently caressed her soft dark hair.

"Alistair?" she said sleepily. She slowly sat up. "Alistair!" She jumped onto the bed and wrapped her arms around him. "You are okay, thank God you are okay." She held him tightly to her.

"I heard your sweet songs." He nuzzled his face against her hair.

She pulled away from their embrace. "I better go get Tomar and let him know you are awake." She reached up her hands and caressed his face. He was a little pale, but other than that he looked good.

"There is no need to get Tomar."

"Yes there is. Now stay in this bed." Anne hurried over to the door. "Please escort me to where Tomar is," she said to the guard.

Alistair smiled, he was glad she remembered to take the guard with her.

Within moments Anne came back with Tomar right behind her. Tomar gestured to the two female Rundals. Then he helped Alistair out of the bed.

"We will let them clean up your bed then you must lie back down," Tomar said.

"I have to…"

"Do nothing," Anne injected. "Don't worry about the village Demos is taking care of things."

"You must regain your strength," Tomar added. Tomar helped Alistair to the bathing chamber. "I will leave the rest to you. Let me know if you need help," he said to Anne.

Anne removed the covering from Alistair's body then helped him into the bath. She climbed back out and gathered everything needed for a bath.

"Your covering is all wet, why don't you remove it," Alistair said.

Anne set the items down and removed her covering. She entered the warm water and started to soap up the washrag.

"I can bathe myself…" Alistair pulled her to him. "But I do know what you can help me with."

"Alistair…" Anne pushed out of his embrace. "You just woke up from basically a coma and you're horny."

"Mmmm." He licked his lips.

"I don't believe this, there is no way you could possibly want to…"

He grabbed her hand and placed it on his hard cock.

"Okay…I guess you can want to play…but…"

"I want to feel your body on mine." He pulled her to him again.

She could feel that his grasp wasn't as strong as it used to be. He needed to rest not get fucked. "Just lay there." She gently pushed him back so his upper body was leaning against the stone of the bathing pool. She climbed onto his lap and let her pussy sheathed his cock.

"That feels so good," he purred, leaning his head back.

She slowly rode him as she ran her hands over his strong chest. "Alistair," she moaned.

"I will not last long, my female, take your pleasure soon."

She moved her hips faster up and down. She watched his face as he fought to control his orgasm. "Come, my male, let me see your pleasure." Her body quivered as he threw his head back even further and roared his orgasm. She leaned forward and lay against his chest. She felt his strong arms wrap around her.

"I thought…" She started to cry. The relief she felt that he was going to be okay overwhelmed her.

"Shh everything is alright now." He caressed her hair with one hand as he held her to him with his other arm.

"I thought I was never going to feel you like this again. I felt so powerless to stop what was going to happen to you."

"Don't cry…everything is alright." He held her tighter and nuzzled his cheek to the top of her head. "I am sorry you had to go through…I don't want to know the torture they put you through, but I swear I will spend the rest of my life making up to you for my failure to protect you."

"Failure to protect me?" She looked up into his face. "You risked your life to save me."

"I should have…"

"I don't want you to feel like you failed me, don't ever feel that way."

"You have to think less of me. I am your protector and yet…"

"You are my protector and no warrior can even hold a candle to you." She could see her words touched him profoundly.

"I want to be your mate. I want to join with you."

"Join?"

"It is a ceremony in which we promise to love each other forever, we will be able to raise offspring and no other warrior will ever touch you again."

"You want to get married? I think that is what you are saying."

"Married? I don't understand."

"Where a male and female promise to love each other, stand by and take care of each other forever. This is called getting married on my planet."

"Then marry me. I love you more than anything. Marry me Anne."

"Yes Alistair I will marry you." That smile on his face, the glow in his eyes was worth more than any words.

He pulled her back into his embrace and held her tightly. He had never been so happy before, never felt accepted like this. She was home to him.

Anne clutched onto Alistair. She was engaged…she didn't have to think about her answer at all, he is where she belong, be it on Malka or Earth. A warmth surrounded her that she hasn't felt since her parents died. Alistair was home…her home.

ഔഔഔ

Alistair knocked on Tomar's door. A large Rundal male answered the door. "I need to speak with Tomar if he can spare the time," Alistair said.

"Ah Alistair, come in," Tomar called out.

Alistair entered Tomar's chamber. There all sorts of maps and notes lying about.

"I am glad you are feeling better. Demos told me you have been training for a week now."

"I have to get my strength back up to protect my female."

"What wonderful motivation."

"What are you doing?" Alistair looked at the star maps. He had no idea how to read them, but he saw markings all over the map.

"I have wonderful news for Niro."

Alistair could see Tomar's excitement in his eyes.

"Look." Tomar pointed to a planet. "This is the planet Loma."

"Loma?"

"It is so similar to Malka. The scouts I sent have come back." Tomar gestured to the two large Rundal males.

"There are warriors on this planet?"

"Oh yes, but not the warriors you are thinking of."

"I don't understand."

"On Loma the warriors are all female."

"Female! All of them."

"I understand your surprise. It seems on Loma the females are the dominant sex. The males on this planet are like your weaker males. What is even more fascinating is that there is a shortage of males on this planet. Just like there is a shortage of females on this planet. It seems like your two planets could really help each other out. The only problem is the females seemed to only want the smaller males and I am not sure if the males on this planet would take to having females who are just as skilled as they are in battle."

"Are the rulers female as well?"

"Yes."

"Have you told anyone else about the planet?"

"I told Nina and Demos, both of them have volunteered to go as representatives of Malka. Of course I must talk with Niro first. Robin will be most thrilled about this news. The weaker males on Malka will be cherished on Loma. Oh but listen to me rattle on. What did you want to see me about?"

"I wanted to ask a great favor of you...I ask that you allow me to take Anne back to Earth now. I know Niro said six months, but I don't think my female can wait that long. You can leave us on Earth and come back and pick us up when you send the other ship in five months."

"What about joining the clans?"

"Demos can handle it. Besides...these people see me as a half-breed, which makes them reluctant to follow me. I tried to tell Niro this, but he won't listen."

"Demos is a good man. However he will be biased to the Larmat people. Nina will help him." Tomar started pacing. Alistair has never asked anything of anyone before, so what he asked of Tomar must be very important. And Alistair is right the Larmat and Dascon people do see him as a half-breed. It wasn't fair, but it was the way it was. Niro is trying too hard to change things too fast. You can't change people's prejudice overnight.

"I have to take Anne back to Earth. She needs to find her parent's killers. I have to find a way to make this happen."

"I have an idea, but I can't guarantee that you won't feel Niro's anger when you return."

"I will endure any punishment Niro deems worthy. I have to do this for my female."

"I think you should appoint a Larmat warrior to help Demos."

"What?"

"If you choose a Larmat warrior you will show that Niro does mean to join the clans peacefully. With only

Demos as acting leader of the Larmat clan I am sure they would only think that Niro means to force them to comply."

"I wish Niro was still here."

"Don't worry I will inform Niro what has happened when I head back to the Dascon village."

"Then you will help me."

"If you can get Demos to agree to a Larmat warrior as co-leader of the Larmat clan."

"I will do it."

"These two will take you to Earth." He gestured to the two large Rundal males. "Their ship is just outside this city. It is very small and very fast so you will have to be put to sleep for the journey."

"Alright. Thank you Tomar." Alistair hurried from the room.

Alistair headed straight for the meeting room. He knew Demos would be in there today. He burst open the door and walked straight over to Demos.

"What has happened?" Demos said.

"What I am about to ask of you I know it will be hard for you to accept. I need to choose a Larmat warrior to co-lead with you."

"What?!"

"Please hear me out. I have to take Anne back to Earth now. It is so very important to her. The only way Tomar will take us there is if you agreed to co-lead with a Larmat warrior."

"Hell no," Demos grumbled. "If a Larmat warrior gets even a little power I am sure a rebellion will fire up again."

"Demos..." Nina walked over to him. "It is important to Anne to go back to Earth. Wouldn't you give me what I needed?"

"Of course I would."

"Then why won't you help Alistair give his female what she needs."

"Niro ordered you to rule these people, Alistair."

"Tomar will explain to Niro what has happen and I will endure any punishment Niro gives. I need to do this for my female."

"Which Larmat warrior?"

"Only one name pops into my mind…Mace."

"You ask too much Alistair," Demos growled.

"He believes Niro's words. He could have killed Anne but instead he saved her. He wants peace just like Niro does."

"I think I see where Tomar is going with this," Nina said. She gently grabbed Demos' arm. "If the Larmat people see a Dascon warrior ruling along side of a Larmat warrior what better gesture could there be. They would believe Niro's words of peace."

Demos remained silent.

"These people will never accept me. They see me only as some half-breed. I believe many of them are insulted that Niro put such an abomination as their leader."

"You doubt Niro."

"Of course not, but he doesn't hear what these people say. I have told Niro my thoughts about this."

"I see what Niro wanted to accomplish by appointing you as the ruler of the Larmat people. If they could look beyond what you were and see what a fine warrior you are, then they would easily accept peace with the Dascon, for clearly Niro had already look passed the fact that your parents came from two different clans. What I wonder is why you haven't looked beyond it."

"Demos…" Nina quietly said.

"Why Alistair?"

"Most days I don't think about it. Sometimes it is hard to ignore the whispers and strange looks, especially now that I have a female. I have to think what will she endure once she is joined with me? What will my offspring endure? If you won't help me Demos I will go to Niro and tell him that I am taking my female back to Earth to give her what she needs."

"I will agree to allow that Larmat warrior to help me rule."

"Thank you Demos." Alistair hurried from the room.

"Demos, I know it will be hard for you to do this. I am so very proud of you." Nina wrapped her arms around one of his.

"We have endured whispers and stares. It takes every ounce of my willpower not to slay every one of them. I know how much you want a child and it tears me up to hear those idiots snicker and gossip. I know what Alistair feels like. I would do anything to give you what you needed. I am sorry Nina that I can't give you a child."

"Don't say that it is not your fault." Nina looked up into his face. "Tomar said we are both healthy and should be able to have children. Sometimes these things take some time. I don't care what people say about us, let them talk. And when our daughter grows up and kicks the crap out of their sons then we will have the last laugh."

"A daughter." Demos smiled.

"Well of course. You make me so very happy and proud Demos, a female couldn't ask for more."

"My flower." Demos kissed the top of her head.

Chapter Thirteen

Anne eagerly awaited Alistair's return. All he told her was that he had some very important things to take care of today. Her body craved his. Every time she thinks about his strong body and glorious cock her body would heat up.

She was startled when the door opened.

"What is wrong?" Alistair asked as he entered the room.

"I missed you today."

Alistair smiled at her then his body instantly became aroused seeing that seductive look in her eyes.

"Please sit down on the bed and promise you won't move."

"Why?"

"Just do it."

Alistair did as she asked. She started to hum a most sultry melody. Alistair lowered his hands down to the bed and gripped the edge tightly when she started to sway her hips.

"You have to sit there. Promise me."

"Anything." His eyes couldn't leave her hands as they journeyed down her body to the rhythm of the sultry melody. Slowly, painfully slowly she undid the ties to her covering. As her hips swayed her covering slipped from her body. Alistair gripped the edge of the mattress tighter. His cock was so hard it began to ache.

Anne slowly walked over to him still humming the delicious melody. He reached up to grab her. "Don't touch yet." She playfully slapped his hands away. She unhurriedly came to her knees before him. She looked into his eyes as she licked her lips then she removed his loincloth. She lowered her head down and took his cock into her mouth—still she hummed her sexy melody.

Alistair could feel her humming vibrate against his cock. He went to reach for her head but again she playfully slapped his hands away.

"Sit still, my male," she said as her tongue flicked over the head of his cock. She kept her eyes locked with his as she swallowed his massive cock still humming.

"I can't take too much of this. I am going to spill my seed," he groaned.

His cock popped from her mouth. "You're not coming yet." She stood up and began her sexy dance again.

His hands ached to touch her. He needed to bury his cock deeply in her, wanted to taste her, to lick her until she screamed.

She pushed him down onto the mattress then turned around. She straddled his hips giving him a nice view of her ass. Slowly she rubbed her pussy against his cock as her hand kneaded his balls gently.

"I can take no more female," he growled. He grabbed her hips and rolled over pinning her under him. He reached down and eased his cock into her as he laid on top of her.

"That's it Alistair fill me, oh yes fill me," she purred. She loved feeling his body covering hers, loved his hard cock pumping in and out of her. After a few moments she felt him prop himself up with his arms. He reached one of his arms under her and lifted her hips up. Her body trembled for she knew what was next. She held her breath in anticipation. She felt his teeth sink into her shoulder. She heard his growls and grunts as he rode her faster.

"Yes, yesssss," she purred. Her whole body shuddered from her orgasm. As she laid there dizzy with pleasure she could hear him roar out his orgasm. He slowly pulled his cock out and then lay down on the bed.

She rolled over then propped herself up on her elbow as she looked into his handsome face. He looked so sated.

"Why do you look at me this way?" he said, seeing the puzzled look on her face.

"First I want to say that was wonderful. But..."

"You can tell me anything. Did I not please you? I thought you took your pleasure." Alistair sat up quickly.

"You did please me very much so, in fact. It's just that I was talking with Nina this afternoon and well...this is kind of embarrassing maybe I shouldn't say anything."

"What is it? Please tell me."

"Nina told me that when a warrior is teased too much that well...they turn into this wild thing...you know...they have to come several times before they stop."

"Oh..." Alistair looked away from her.

"Alistair, maybe I didn't tease you enough. I..."

"Your dance...your touches...you teased me I could barely stand it I wanted you so much."

She didn't like the almost hurt tone to his voice.

"The Larmat warriors don't have this sexual frenzy as the Dascon warriors do. Since I am part Larmat I am unable to obtain this frenzy."

"Oh, Alistair I am so sorry." She gently touched his back. She was unsure of what to do. She hurt him, oh God that was never her intention.

Alistair turned around and looked at her. "You don't have to apologize, it's me who should. I am sorry I have disappointed you."

"It's just I don't see you like these people. You are my male that's all I see. It was stupid of me not to talk with a Larmat female first."

He cupped her cheek in his hand and smiled at her. This lightened her heart immediately. "My female," he said gently, caressing her cheek. "I have most exciting news for you." He wanted to change the subject so she wouldn't have to think about what just happened.

"Really, what is it?" She grabbed a blanket and wrapped it around herself as he reached down and put back on his loincloth. He sat down next to her.

"We will be leaving for Earth tomorrow."

"What?!"

"I have arranged with Tomar to have one of his ships take us to Earth. When the other ship comes in five months they will pick us up and bring us back."

"Is this what you have been doing all day?"

"Yes."

"But...what about all the important things you have to do?"

"Seeing to your happiness is the only important thing I must do."

"What about the village?"

"Demos and Mace will take care of that. Now we must prepare for our journey. Tomar said we will be put to sleep while we are in the ship."

"I wasn't put to sleep when they brought me here."

"That was a much bigger ship. The one we will be taking is smaller and travels much faster. It will only take a few days to reach Earth."

"Holy shit that will be fast, I am kind of glad we will be asleep."

"Me too." He chuckled. "I am looking forward to seeing your world."

"I can't wait to show it to you. But..."

"Finding your parent's killers is our most important priority."

"Thank you Alistair. Thank you so much."

"Your happiness is so very important to me, my female." Alistair opened his arms and she fell into his embrace. "I will do what I can to help you. When you find who was responsible for your parents' death I will kill them for you."

Anne wanted to tell him not to kill anyone, but in her heart she couldn't do it. Why should her parents' murderers be allowed to live? Wasn't it justice? Eye for an eye.

Chapter Fourteen

Anne was so groggy as she felt the rubbery, scaly skin of a Rundal rub against her face.

"Are you okay?" She heard a very gentle male voice ask.

She slowly sat up and looked into the face of the Rundal male. "I am okay, I think. Alistair…"

"He is waking up." The Rundal male helped her out of the pod she was in. This ship was much smaller than the one she was brought to Malka with. There was only the cockpit and this chamber that held a few pods and some supply crates.

"My things?" She looked frantically around her. She brought the book that Hakan had created for Alistair. She hoped that he would read it while they were on Earth.

"Don't worry, I put yours and Alistair's belongs in a pod."

"Anne."

"Alistair." She smiled at him. The Rundal male stepped out of the way and let Alistair go to her.

"My head is still swimming," Alistair said.

"Mine too."

Anne felt the blast of cool fresh air enter the chamber as the Rundal male opened the hatch. It was dark outside so she could see very little. Alistair helped her out of the ship, then he looked around. He gazed up at the stars sparkling in the night sky.

"Beautiful," he whispered.

Anne recognized the area they were in. It was the small park that was a block or so from her home. She looked at Alistair standing there in his loincloth with his large sword strapped to his back.

"We will return in five months time," the Rundal male said.

"Thank you." Alistair bowed his head in a show of respect for the Rundal.

Anne looked behind her and watched the ship take off. Within a moment it was gone.

"Alistair we better hurry up and get to my house." She couldn't let anyone see him like this. Someone was going to call the cops. Hell she would if she saw a very large, half-naked man with a sword on his back.

She grabbed Alistair's hand and led him to her house. Thankfully everyone was still asleep. She would have to remember to buy him some clothes. Where was she going to find clothes that would fit his large muscular body? She grabbed the spare key that she had tape under her mailbox and opened the door. She grabbed the huge pile of mail then entered the house.

"What are those?" Alistair said, looking at the mail.

"Just mail…umm…letters…writings." She saw that he understood.

Alistair slowly walked through the house. Anne enjoyed the look of wonderment on his face. He walked into the kitchen and let his eyes wander everywhere.

"This is where meals are prepared."

"How? There is no fire."

Anne lit the stove. Alistair reached out his hand to touch the flame. "Don't do that you will burn yourself."

"There is no wood."

"It uses gas…don't worry I will cook the meals for us."

Alistair walked back into the living room. He could see his reflection off of the big screen TV.

"Here let me turn that on." Anne grabbed the remote and clicked on the TV. Alistair jumped back and drew his sword. "Calm down Alistair, it won't hurt you." She quickly turned it off.

He slowly sheathed his sword. "Is this how you felt when you saw Malka?"

"How do you feel?"

"Overwhelmed."

"Yeah that's pretty much how I felt."

Alistair continued walking through the house. He was like a lost child in an amusement park, thrilled and at the same time frightened. He headed into her bedroom. He pushed on the mattress then he grabbed the blanket. He brought it up to his nose and smelt it. "Mmm, it smells like you." He saw the silky sheets and couldn't resist running his hands over it. "This feels like you." Alistair turned toward her. He untied his loin- cloth and let it fall to the ground. He reached for her and tore her covering from her body. He lifted her up into his arms then slowly lowered her down onto the bed. The coolness of the sheets against the contrast of her warm skin felt so good to him. He grabbed his cock and slowly eased it inside her.

"Slowly, Alistair," she purred. She reached up and pulled him down to her. She wanted to taste his lips, feel his body against hers. She tangled her hands in his hair as her lips devoured his. He groaned and buried his cock to the hilt in her. Her tongue gently probed his mouth causing him to moan deeply. He gently sucked on her offered tongue wanting to taste, tease and excite her. He felt her hips start to move, but he reached his hands down and pinned her hips to the bed. He had to be careful that his body weight wouldn't crush her. He stuck his tongue deeply into her mouth letting it flick across the roof of her mouth. Her tongue flicked the underside of his causing a rush of pleasure to race through his body. He reached under her and grabbed her ass as he started to slowly thrust. He gently kneaded her ass with each thrust of his cock. His tongue flicked in her mouth then on her lips.

"Alistair," she moaned.

Her body felt so good pressed against his. He could hear her labor breaths, but she didn't protest about the weight of his body on hers.

"Yes...ah....yes..." she moaned loudly. His body moving against hers, oh she could feel each thrust of his cock going slowly inch-by-inch in and out of her. His hot kisses, the weight of him on her. "Alistair...ALISTAIR!" she cried out.

Hearing her scream his name brought him right over the edge of bliss. He drove his cock hard into her as he spilled his seed deeply into her. He laid on her for a brief moment and then slowly rolled off of her. The coolness of the silky sheets felt good on his hot skin as he lay their enjoying his afterglow.

"Mmm, that was soooo good," she purred as she snuggled up against him.

"Oh yes," he said, breathing hard.

"It will be dawn soon. Alistair..."

"When you pause it is something I don't want to hear or you are unsure of what I will think about it."

"What?"

"You always pause what you are saying when you are afraid of what I might think. You needn't ever fear me."

"I just don't want to hurt you by saying something stupid. I was just going to say you have to stay in this house until I get you some new clothes...coverings."

"Why?"

Anne rolled out of bed and grabbed the fashion magazine she had on the nightstand. She handed it to him. "This is how people dress on Earth."

He sat up then flipped through the pages. "You have good creators on Earth," he said, looking at the photos of the men and women in the magazine.

"Creators?"

"These pictures look as though they could walk out of this book. Your creators must have very talented hands."

"Oh…these are photos not drawings. I will show you later what I mean. But you see how the males are dressed?"

"This weaker male?" Alistair said, pointing at the skinny male model.

"Well on Earth a lot of men look like that. Males come in all shapes and sizes here on Earth. I have to buy you some clothes, you can't walk around in your loincloth and you most certainly can't carry your sword."

"What? I never go anywhere without my sword."

"Trust me Alistair. Things are so much different here than they are on Malka."

"I trust you Anne. But you can't go walking around without me."

"I will be safe I promise." She could see the uneasiness in his eyes.

"This makes me feel uneasy…but I should follow the rules and customs of your planet."

"Thank you Alistair."

Alistair flipped through the magazine. "Is everyone this frail on this planet?"

"Frail…no, we Earthlings come in all shapes, sizes and colors." She grabbed her robe. "Follow me."

Alistair pulled on his loincloth and followed her to the living room.

"Sit." She patted the spot of the sofa next to her. She clicked on the TV. She flipped through the different channels letting him see the different kinds of people.

"Wait," Alistair said, looking at the images of war shown on the news. "Your clans are warring?"

"Yeah unfortunately." Anne clicked off the TV.

"There are so many different kinds of males and females, so many females."

"Didn't Tomar explain the way Earth works?"

"He said there were many females and that the warriors on this planet were smaller than us. He might have told Hakan or Niro more about this planet."

"I have to get dress." Anne quickly went to the bedroom to change then she hurried back into the living room. "I am going to buy you some clothes then I am going to stop by the police station. I might be gone for a while. Promise me you will stay in this house."

"I don't know. I don't like the fact you will be all by yourself."

"I will be okay. Please promise you won't leave the house."

"If this will make you happy."

"Thank you Alistair." She bent over and kissed him softly. "I will try and be back as soon as I can. I will bring back something for us to eat."

Alistair watched her walk out the door. He didn't like this. What if she needed him? He would have no idea on how to find her. He saw the door open back up and Anne hurrying back in.

"This is a phone." She gestured to the phone on the side table. "When it makes a ringing noise...here let me show you." She pulled out her cell phone and dialed her house number. Alistair jumped to his feet when the phone rang. Anne picked up the phone and handed it to Alistair. "Hold it like that. See you can hear my voice. I will call you every hour so you know I am alright." She took the receiver from him and sat it back down. "You have to put it back just like this. Now you will know that I am alright."

She smiled seeing the puzzled look on his face. "Remember you promised to stay in the house."

Alistair nodded his head and watched her leave again. He wasn't sure that he liked this planet. There were so many strange things and he hasn't even left her house yet. He couldn't wear his clothes or carry his sword. Everything was strange to him. He sat down on the sofa and just stared at the blank TV screen.

಄಄಄

Anne drove to the police station first. She was disappointed that there were no new leads. She remembered the papers that were all over her kitchen table and on the floor. She quickly pulled out her cell phone and called her house. She heard the phone click then silence.

"Alistair?"

"Anne?"

"I am just calling to say I am okay. Plus there are writings in the cooking area. Would you mind picking them up and placing them on the table?"

"Alright. Hurry back."

"I will Alistair." She hung up the phone. She could hear the lost tone in his voice. She couldn't afford to leave him alone for too long. He did promise he would stay in the house, but still.

She drove around everywhere looking for clothes that would fit him. Finally she found a big and tall shop. She explained to the clerk that she needed something that would fit a six foot six very muscular man. Thankfully he was very helpful and they managed to find three very nice outfits that would fit Alistair. She had to admit she was most eager to see Alistair in a pair of jeans and tight fitting shirt. She knew he would look quite yummy.

She headed home and Alistair about tackled her when she entered the house. He held her so tightly to him she could hardly breathe.

"You are going to have to let me go, Alistair." She gasped for air when he set her down.

"What are those?" he said, pointing to the bag.

"These are for you." She grabbed his hand and led him to the bedroom. "Take off your covering."

Alistair removed his loincloth and stood there naked. Anne grabbed a pair of jeans, T-shirt and some underwear from the bag. She turned toward him and stopped. He looked so good standing there naked. Her eyes slowly wandered down his muscular body. She watched as his large cock started to grow hard, she couldn't look away.

"I am yours to take, my female," Alistair whispered in his soft deep voice.

Anne dropped the clothes and walked over to him. She grabbed his hard cock firmly in her hand, his cock so thick she couldn't wrap her small hand completely around it. Her other hand wandered across his chiseled stomach and chest. She wanted to explore his beautiful body and as if he knew exactly what she wanted he stood completely still, allowing her to do as she will with him.

He was magnificent, what female wouldn't want to be with this man. She removed her hand from his cock and let it wander up his chest then across his broad shoulders. She moved around to the back of him and let her hands wandered down his back, she traced the outline of the "V" his back and shoulders made. She brought both hands to his waist then slowly she ran her hands down to his firm beautiful ass.

"You are such a beautiful male, Alistair," she purred.

She came down to a squatting position behind him and allowed her hands to wander down his strong legs.

Every inch of him was firm and strong. She gently urged him to spread his legs, he did so without hesitation. She turned herself around, grabbed his strong legs and positioned herself under him.

Alistair felt the softness of her hair brush across his balls. His anticipation grew. He moaned softly as her tongue began to lick his balls and the tender spot just behind them.

"Stroke your cock for me, Alistair," she said between licks.

He reached down and grabbed his cock firmly in his hand—slowly he stroked his cock as she continued to lap at his balls.

"Faster Alistair," she moaned. She took as much of his tender skin as she could into her mouth and gently sucked.

"Female…" he growled. He stroked his cock faster and faster. He could feel her sucking on his balls. She tried to take more and more of his sensitive flesh into her mouth. Her muffled moans brought him right to the edge then she stopped.

"Wait, my male…I want you to fill my mouth with your sweet cum." She licked his balls briefly then pulled herself to the front of him.

He looked down seeing her squatting there in front him. She reached over and grabbed his cock and started to help him stroke at it. His eyes locked on her beautiful opened mouth.

"Feed me, my male," she purred.

He felt the cum surge up his shaft then the intense explosion of his orgasm. He moaned loudly watching his cum fill her mouth. He stroked his cock firmly wanting her to eat every drop of his nectar. His eyes were mesmerized watching her lick her lips then the head of his cock. When she released him he reached down and grabbed her. He lifted her up until her pussy was right in front of his face.

Her hands gripped the back of his head to steady herself. Her body trembled as he lightly blew on her pussy lips.

"Alistair," she moaned when he buried his face in her pussy, licking and sucking, devouring her like a ravenous man. He gripped her ass firmly making her rub her pussy all over his face.

She gasped when he slowly fell back onto the bed. He held her firmly to him urging her to rub her pussy hard against his face while he continued to lick her. She arched back as her orgasm washed over her. She lifted her hips slightly needing her sensitive clit to rest. He knew this and concentrated his licking at her opening. His tongue darted in and out as he lapped up her sweet juice. He scooted her forward a little so his tongue could reach her ass.

"Alistair…" she moaned, surprised by the sensation of his tongue circling around her rosebud. His nose went up into her, she tried to raise her hips afraid she might be hurting him but he held her in place. His tongue circling around and around as he moved his face just slightly letting his nose rubbed her inside, the combination of sensations quickly brought on her second orgasm.

She tried to climb off his face.

"Oh no you don't, I am not done tasting you." He lifted her up. She was surprised that he was able to lift her up and turn her around with such ease. He gripped her hips and pulled her down on his face again. He moved her hips back and forth wanting her to rub her pussy on his face.

He reached back and slapped her ass. "Rub yourself against me, female. I want you to cover my face with your juice." He slapped her ass again when she didn't start right away.

Anne leaned forward a little placing her hands on his chest to balance herself. She started to rub her pussy back and forth. She gasped when he slapped her ass again. She rubbed faster and harder against his face. His muffled growls told her she was giving him what he wanted. Her third orgasm rocked her so hard she fell forward.

"I am not done yet, female." He sucked lightly on her pussy lips.

She reached down and grabbed his cock.

"Alistair I want you to fuck me, please Alistair."

"Not yet." He flipped them over so now he was on top. He buried his tongue back in her pussy, darting it in and out of her opening in a slow steady rhythm. He growled feeling her lick at his cock.

"Ooo...umm...Alistair!" she cried out her fourth orgasm. "Please fuck me...please."

He climbed off of her and just sat there looking at her.

"Please Alistair, I need your cock deep inside me."

That look of want...of need on her face excited him. He pulled her to him and took one of her breasts into his mouth. He sat back against the headboard. The head of his cock poised right at her opening. He could feel her juice drip on his cock. She was so wet, so eager for him. He held her in place denying her his cock as he suckled on her breasts. He could feel her body tremble, oh sweet anticipation.

"Alistair..." she said breathily.

He looked up into her beautiful face as her nipple popped from his mouth. With one strong thrust he buried his cock to the hilt in her warm, wet pussy.

"Alistair!!" she cried out.

He released her hips and allowed her to ride him. His hands wandered over her soft body as she moved up and down in a frantic pace. He watched her face wanting her to take her pleasure before he did. But the intensity in which she was riding him quickly brought him right to the edge of bliss.

"Female...take your pleasure." His deep voice excited her as she moved faster and faster.

She looked into his face and watched him struggle to contain his orgasm.

"Come...my male," she purred.

"AHHHH!!!" he cried. He gripped her hips and drove his cock hard and deep as his cum spurted into her. He came and came as his orgasm seemed to last forever. He could hear her sweet moans as she joined him on this wave of ecstasy.

She collapsed into his embrace. "Alright what were we doing before this amazing fuck?" she said between breaths.

"I can't think at the moment."

"Oh yeah, I remember I was going to dress you." She slowly climbed off of him and dragged herself out of bed. She reached down and grabbed the clothes off the floor. "I will let you dress yourself." She explained to him how to put on the clothes. She told him how to use the shower. She left the room and headed for the guest room to take a shower.

When she was finished with her shower she went to the kitchen to get some coffee. Her body felt deliciously used. She couldn't help but smile. She stopped and looked at the stack of papers neatly placed on the kitchen table. He had done what she asked. She poured herself a cup of coffee then sat down and looked at the pile of papers. A sense of guilt swept over her. Up until she met Alistair her parents' murder consumed every thought she had, so much so she had to quit school. Alistair gave her a respite, when she was with him thoughts of revenge and profound sadness disappeared. Was this right? How could she enjoy herself like this when she still hasn't found the person responsible for her parents' death? Just when it looked like the guilt would consume her Alistair walked into the room.

"Did I put the covering on right?" he asked.

Anne looked over to him. The clothes fit him perfectly. His long, light brown hair was still tied back like he had it. Damn he looked so good.

"You look perfect." She smiled. "When we go out today, please do what I say alright. The laws on Earth are much different than on Malka.

"I will do as you say." Alistair didn't like these coverings. They were very uncomfortable and how was he supposed to fight in these. He walked over to the kitchen table and grabbed his sword. He was about to strap it on his back when Anne stopped him.

"You can't wear your sword."

"How am I supposed to protect you without it?"

"Since you are much bigger than most of the males on this planet I don't think you will have a problem with that. Alistair you must listen to me. If you hurt someone on Earth you can go to jail." She saw the puzzled look on his face. "Um, the leaders on this planet will punish you."

"Why? I would be only protecting my female."

"They won't see it that way." She glanced back at the pile of papers.

"I read your writings while you were gone. I have thought up a battle plan."

"What? You can read…" Then she remembered that the Larmat people's writing was very similar to hers. If she could figure out their words of course Alistair could figure out hers.

"I hope it was okay that I read your writing? I wanted to help you. The more I know about what has happened the easier it was to figure out a battle plan."

She could see in his eyes just how much he wanted to help her. He knew how very important this was to her. "What have you come up with?"

"While I don't understand what difference it makes that your parents had different skin tones...do you have a drawing of your parents?"

"Yes." She quickly got up and went to the living room. She grabbed the photo from the bookshelf and went back into the kitchen. "My parents," she said, handing him the picture.

Alistair looked at the picture of the very happy couple. The love they had for each other showed in their eyes. "Your mother was very beautiful. You have your father's smile."

Anne broke down and started to cry. Alistair immediately jumped up and took her into his arms. "If the people who have done this heinous crime are still watching you, they will see me with you. If skin tone means so much to them, my lighter skin should enrage them."

Anne looked up at him. He gently wiped away her tears. "Then I will catch them and kill them for you."

"Why would they still be watching me? I have been gone for over a month."

"It said in your writings that you believe these people were stalking your parents, which means they must live in the radius of where your parents traveled. There are many huts in this village so tracking them down will prove most difficult, but not impossible. You will take me to where your parents would have traveled together. These people will see us and start stalking us."

"Alistair..." His plan was so simple, but yet so brilliant at the same time. But these people will have guns. Alistair will not know what a gun is. "Their weapons are much stronger than your sword. We will have to let the police help us."

"I don't need help protecting my female."

"You don't understand. On Earth we have weapons that even a weaker male could take you down with."

"Show me this weapon."

She knew this would be the only way to make him understand. She knew several of the police officers well—maybe they would help her out, but how to do this without drawing attention to Alistair?

"Alright I will show you. I know people who have this weapon." Anne gathered up her purse and car keys. "Are you ready?"

"Yes."

"Remember you promise to do what I say."

"I will."

They headed out of her house and to her car. She climbed in and saw Alistair was still standing in the driveway looking at the car. She climbed back out of the car.

"What's wrong?"

"What is that?"

"Let's say it's like your conja." She smiled seeing him slowly walk over to the car. He placed his hand on the warm metal.

"It's not alive."

"It's kind of like a mix of your conja and a Rundal's ship." She climbed back in the car and reached over to open his door. He hesitantly climbed into the passenger seat. She pressed the button to make the seat go all the way back. She reached across him and put his seat belt on, then she put hers on. When she pulled out he gripped the door and the dashboard.

"You go on a ship that travels faster than the speed of light and fly on the back of a conja without blinking an eye and yet a car freaks you out." She chuckled.

She drove him everywhere her parents would have gone, then she took him to one of her parent's favorite restaurant.

They walked inside. Alistair looked around as they waited to be seated. There were many weaker males with females sitting at the various tables.

Anne grabbed his hand when the waiter showed them to their table. Alistair glared down at the much smaller male when he got a little too close to Anne for Alistair's liking. The waiter quickly went away.

"Alistair please sit down." Anne gestured to the chair across from her.

"There are too many males looking at you. How did these weaker males obtain the right to be with the females?"

"There are plenty of females on Earth remember. You have to stop glaring at every man that comes near me. You about gave our waiter a heart attack. On Earth it's okay that other males get near females, just as long as they are polite."

Anne opened up the menu. Alistair looked around the restaurant. A blonde hair female sitting with a weaker male smiled seductively at him.

Anne looked up when Alistair made a strange noise.

"What's wrong?"

"Why is that female looking at me that way in front of her male?"

"She thinks your hot looking. That may be her brother or friend she is with. You better get use to females looking at you like that. You are a very handsome looking male."

"You are my female. I don't want other females looking at me like that."

Anne smiled at him.

"Are you ready to order?" a female waitress asked. Obviously Alistair scared the male waiter too much.

"Yeah we will have the steak dinners."

She enjoyed watching Alistair as he looked at everything. She wondered if he got the same enjoyment when she was on Malka and everything was new to her?

After a little while the waitress came with their steaks.

"This is a fork and knife, it's pretty much like your eating utensils on Malka." She watched as Alistair enjoyed his meal.

When they were finished she paid for the meal then explained to Alistair about money as they headed back to the car. She took him home then they walked to the park, just like her parents did every evening after dinner. Being with him she was able to enjoy the good memories of her parents. Talking about them to him felt good. Most of all seeing him look at everything with such wonderment lifted her heart. She was relieved that he did keep his promise and did as she asked, though she knew it was hard for him.

When they went home he made love to her. He fell asleep in her arms. She pulled the tie from his long hair as he slept with his head cradled to her breasts and his arms wrapped around her. She leisurely let her fingers run through his silky hair. Today he gave her a special gift and he didn't even know he had. He gave her what she needed to start the healing process.

Chapter Fifteen

It had been a month now since Alistair was on Earth with her. They made sure to be seen together in public, going to all the places her parents use to go to.

Anne cleaned the kitchen as she watched Alistair practice with his sword in the living room. He made sure to move everything far out of the way, especially after he had accidentally chopped her coffee table in half. He had to modify his training to make use of the small space. When he wasn't outdoors with her, he wore his loincloth. He hated the Earth coverings and wore them as little as possible. She could sense he missed Malka, she had to admit in a way she did too.

The phone rang startling Alistair. She laughed and walked over to answer it.

"I told you bitch to leave and not to come back," an angry voice said.

Alistair quickly walked over to her when he saw that frightened look on her face. She raised her hand to stop him.

"I know you are listening. Did you not learn your lesson when your parents died? Do you want to die? Who is that white man I see you hanging all over?"

Then the phone clicked.

"Anne," Alistair quietly said.

"It was the same man who used to call and harass my parents."

"Your police can tell us where he is now, can't they?"

"Unfortunately no, he didn't stay on the line long enough."

The phone rang again this time Alistair answered it. "What do you want?" Alistair growled.

"Are you the freak's white boyfriend? Stay away from her unless you want to die too."

"Come here and show yourself."

"You are begging to get shot aren't you? Why don't you find yourself a nice white woman?"

"Why don't you come here and say such words directly to me instead of cowering in the shadows?"

"You are going to die too."

"I doubt that. I think you will be the one who ends up dead."

Anne couldn't believe that Alistair was keeping the man on the line. Something she could never do. She was always too afraid to talk.

"I will kill that bitch right in front of you for that."

"Stop talking and just do it."

"Let's see how brave you are when I have my gun in your face. Shit!"

Alistair heard the phone click. He set it back down and looked at Anne.

"Alistair, I think you kept him on the line long enough for the police to track him."

"If this is true he will quickly leave. I must take you somewhere safe."

"No, I will stay here with you. You remember what the police showed you. You saw just how powerful a weapon a gun is."

"Yes. Trust me Anne." No strange weapon was going to keep him from protecting her. Let the male come. Once Alistair killed him Anne will be able to heal from her loss.

The phone rang again this time making Anne jump. She quickly answered it and was relieved to hear Frank on the other end. Alistair did manage to keep the man on the line long enough. The police knew who it was now. She thanked Frank from the bottom of her heart. If he hadn't put the trace back on her phone they would never have found the man. He told her to sit tight and that he was sending a squad car over right away.

"Who is Frank?"

"The policeman I introduce you to at the police station. He was the one who has helped me so much."

"Then I must thank this male."

It was a long night as Alistair waited up ready to challenge the male, but he never came. Anne had to admit she was relieved. Alistair was a grand warrior on his planet, but did he really understand the destructive power of a gun?

In the morning both of them were startled by the knock on the door. Anne looked out the window and was relieved to see Frank on the doorstep. "Just a minute," she called out. "Alistair please go change into your Earth coverings."

"I will not leave your side."

"It's okay, it's just Frank."

Alistair hurried upstairs to change.

Anne opened the door and let Frank in.

"We caught them Anne…we finally got 'em."

Anne felt like she couldn't breathe. For so long she waited for this moment.

"They were a couple of skin heads who lived out by the park. We raided the apartment and found all sorts of hate paraphernalia. You wouldn't have known it by looking at the two, they looked like two average men."

"Where are they I want to see them."

"When we raided the apartment the men open fired. We were forced to kill them. Luckily only one officer got wounded and thankfully not seriously."

"They're dead…"

"Hello Alistair," Frank said as Alistair came down the steps dressed in a pair of jeans and a white dress shirt.

Alistair went to Anne and wrapped his arm around her.

"They won't hurt you anymore Anne. Now you can find closure."

"Thank you Frank." She was having trouble letting all of this sink in. She felt Alistair pull her closer as if letting her borrow some of his strength.

"I am in your debt," Alistair said to Frank.

Anne couldn't move, she just watched Frank leave. It was over. Her parents' killers were dead and yet she felt numb.

Alistair scooped her up in his arms and carried her upstairs. He gently laid her down on the bed and sat next to her. "Now you can heal," he said softly as he stroked her hair.

"I wanted to tell them…"

"I know…then tell them now."

"What?"

"Say what you wanted to tell them. Their spirits will hear."

Anne slowly sat up. Her thoughts were muddled. "My parents were two of the most kind and loving people…why did you take them away from me? Just because they didn't share a skin color, what did that matter? I was born out of love, my parents loved and cherished me, no one could have asked for better parents. I am not an abomination but a lucky person who had two wonderful, giving parents. The lessons they taught me will never leave me, you can never take my memories away from me." Her body trembled.

"You are not an abomination, my female." Alistair stroked her face. "Your parents must have been amazing to raise such a wonderful female."

Anne looked into his handsome face. "You are not an abomination either Alistair." She reached over and pulled the book Hakan made for Alistair from her nightstand. "You have given me closure Alistair, made me feel alive again. Let me help you find closure." She handed him the book.

Alistair took the book from her.

"I am going to rest now. The emotions of this day have exhausted me. Please read that book Alistair."

Alistair kissed her gently on the forehead then covered her with the blanket. He watched as she drifted off to sleep. He went over and sat down on the chair in the corner. He stared at the cover of the book for what seemed like an eternity. Slowly he opened the book and began to read.

ౠౠౠ

Anne woke up in the middle of the night. She was startled seeing Alistair just sitting in the chair staring out the window with his sword lying in his lap.

"Alistair?" She slowly climbed out of bed.

"All this time I thought my mother made up stories about my father. She wanted so much to protect me. I could barely remember him. But when I read that book I could see him."

Anne walked over to him and knelt down beside him.

"I now remember this sword. It was always strapped to his back. He was so big, so strong looking and yet he held me so gentle. I remember my mother telling me what a fierce warrior my father was and now all I can remember is how kind his face looked, how his eyes lit up when he played with me. I have his eyes, his smile, his voice and his strength."

Anne placed her hand gently on his leg.

"When he stop coming around I believed he just stopped loving us. I always thought it was because of me that he didn't return. That he finally believed that I was a half-breed and unworthy of love. I watched my mother suffer—saw the countless tears she tried to hide from me. The guilt I felt knowing it was my fault that she lost my father's love. I hated him so much for what he did to my mother. She was the only person through my childhood who loved me. She protected me from the others, shielded me from their venomous words. And he left us…"

Alistair paused, he had to collect himself. He didn't want to cry in front of Anne. He was supposed to be strong. He didn't want to show her any weakness.

"Alistair…" Tears came to Anne's eyes. She could see his pain in his eyes.

"I remember my mother telling me he died. I didn't believe her. I thought she was protecting me again. Now I read this book and see she told me the truth. He gave his life for mine…he did love me. He didn't leave us, he protected us. The same way I would give my life to protect you and our future offspring. And I spent my life hating him…"

"Alistair you were only a child. It would have seemed like he abandoned you when he stop coming to visit."

"I should have trusted in him. I should have believed my mother when she said he had died." Alistair gripped the sword. "I was so afraid to read about my father, afraid that he might have been the awful person that I made him out to be in my mind. And he was not that awful person at all. He was a grand warrior who fell in love with a female captive from another clan. He could have had any Larmat female he wanted and yet he chose my mother. He saved her from being used by the other warriors. When he found out that she carried his child he knew he had to take her away from the Larmat village. His people would have killed me and her. He brought her back to the Dascon village she was from hoping that her people would show some compassion. He couldn't afford to be spotted with my mother, the warriors in the Dascon village would have attacked him. It wasn't because he feared these warriors—he couldn't bear to slay them in front of my mother. She had known some of these warriors since she was a child. And the fact they took her back into their village even when she began to show her pregnancy. They knew a Larmat warrior must have seeded her. Her protector had been slain over a year ago."

"They didn't care."

"Oh they cared but they had no proof. My father wrote in this book that he was glad to see that I had the brownish color hair of the Dascon people. Maybe they would not kill me for being a half-breed. When I was only four my father was caught in my mother's hut, not by a Dascon warrior but a Larmat warrior. A small band of Larmat warriors were raiding the village. Before my father had a chance to kill the four remaining Larmat warriors they escaped. He knew they would report what they found to their leader. Me and my mother were banished a month later from the Dascon village that is when Hakan took us in. My father went to him in the hope that he would take pity on us and protect us, when he knew Hakan would do just that he turned himself over to the Larmat leader."

Anne sat there silently. She could see Alistair trying to contain his emotions. Her heart ached for him.

"My whole life I believe my father didn't want me because I was a half-breed. I believe my mother only tried to make him look good to protect me. He did love me…" Alistair couldn't hold back the tears. The overwhelming mix of emotions, guilt, love, anger…all of it swirled around until he wanted to scream.

"Alistair." Anne removed the sword and climbed onto his lap. She wrapped her arms tightly around him. She felt him latch onto her.

"He loved me so much that he died for me and I spent my whole life hating him." The words broke as he spoke.

"You now know what he felt. How could you back then. Shh…Alistair. He left that book so you would know the truth. He must have known what you would have gone through being different from the others. He wanted you to know who he was in his own words. He must have known what your mother would have gone through to protect you. And that you would find it hard to believe what she was saying about him. You were only a child. If my father left without a word when I was that little I would have probably came to that same conclusion. The important thing now is that you know the truth."

Alistair hugged her tighter. She eased his pain and guilt.

"I know what is like to be different. Luckily on Earth most people are now opened-minded about mixed couples and their children. But there is always ignorant ones who feel that it is wrong. I can't begin to imagine what it is like for you. To have only a handful of people that doesn't look upon you as different. And yet you became a grand warrior just like your father, despite what the others thought about you. Your mother must have been one heck of a female to have raised such a wonderful male. Your father would be so proud of you. Now you know the truth, enjoy the memories of your father and the stories your mother told about him."

She held him tightly and softly sang to him. She needed to ease his pain, needed to bring comfort to him.

They stayed in their embrace until the sun began to rise.

Anne climbed off his lap. She smiled seeing no pain in his eyes. Both of them could begin healing.

"If I remember correctly you did ask me to join with you."

"Yes." He smiled.

"Let's get married here on Earth."

"Would this make you happy?"

"Oh very much so."

"Then we will join through your planet's custom. What do we do?"

"Well first we need to get dress and go apply for a marriage license. I will set up for a justice of the peace to come to this house. He or she is going to think it's strange that you will be wearing a loincloth and a sword, but I don't care I want to marry you with you wearing your Malka coverings."

"How long does this take?"

"A couple of days." She grabbed his hand and led him to the shower. She slowly undressed him then herself. She turned on the shower then gestured for him to join her. She gasped when he lifted her up in his arms then impaled her with his huge cock. He rode her hard and fast pressing her up against the wall as the water sprayed over them. It didn't take long for both of them to reach orgasm.

After about an hour they left to get their marriage license. Anne could only hope that his blood was similar to hers or won't that be hard to explain.

ନ୍ଧନ୍ଧନ୍ଧ

Anne couldn't help but smile seeing the surprised look on the woman's face when Alistair entered the living room wearing his loincloth and having his sword strapped to his back.

Anne wore a Malka covering in a beautiful blue color. She could see Alistair was very pleased with her choice of outfits.

Anne bought them simple gold wedding rings and seeing Alistair slipping the ring on her finger as he said his vows filled her with so much joy. He completed her. She remembered the first time she saw him he wore the exact same outfit he is wearing now. She remembered the instant sexual attraction to him. She wanted not to have any feelings for him, wanted nothing to do with him at first, but now…he was everything to her.

Her hands shook slightly when she placed the ring on his finger. She could hardly recognize her own voice as she repeated the vows. She would love and cherish him forever. She didn't need this ceremony to confirm what she felt for him. This meant so much to him. She could see just how much by just looking in his eyes. After the justice of the peace declared them husband and wife she threw herself in his arms and kissed him deeply. He was hers and she was his forever.

After the woman left Alistair carried Anne up the stairs to her bedroom. He gently laid her down on the bed and slowly, carefully removed her covering. His touches were so tender as he revealed her body to his hungry eyes. She felt so cherished at this moment, just the way he looked at her, touched her. Especially that look in his eyes a mixture of love and admiration, peace and desire. In this moment he told her without words just how very much she meant to him. That she was everything to him as he was to her.

After he had removed her covering he stood up and removed his sword. He got down on his knees and offered her the sword. "I swear to protect and provide for you and our future offspring. I give my body, my heart, my soul to you." Alistair wasn't sure about the sacred words of the joining ceremony. He wasn't taught them. But he had a need to say them to her.

Anne looked at Alistair kneeling there holding out his sword. She got up on her knees and took the sword from his hands. She didn't know what she was supposed to say, but it seemed like her gesture was enough for him. He stood up and removed his loincloth then gently he took his sword from her and set it on the ground beside the bed.

"My female," he whispered. She was his, never did he think he would ever have the honor of being someone's mate. He slowly laid her back down then he climbed on the bed and lay on his side beside her. He let his hand leisurely run down her body, letting his eyes memorize every inch of her. He looked into her eyes. Her beauty was beyond compare. This precious female was his. He would spend his life bringing her pleasure and happiness. He would kill anyone who hurt her or their offspring. Slowly he lowered his head down and captured her lips with his. He kissed her tenderly as his hand continued to explore her body.

She felt the heat of his kiss and was almost disappointed when he moved away. He lowered his mouth down and took her nipple into his mouth. Leisurely he suckled as his fingers circled her clit. She gently caressed his hair as he continued to suckle. His fingers expertly stroked her clit quickly bringing her to the brink of orgasm, but he let her lingering there.

He looked up into her face as he continued to suckle. He growled seeing the pleasure he was bringing her. He let the nipple pop from his mouth then slowly he kissed down her stomach as his fingers continued to stroke and tease her.

She reached down her hands and latched onto his head urging him to go lower. She moaned loudly as he buried his tongue in her pussy. He flicked his tongue over her clit as he buried two fingers deeply in her.

"Alistair," she purred as she moved her hips.

He rammed his fingers in and out of her, faster and faster as he continued to lick her clit. He felt her hips arch up. She was right there, so close to orgasm. He was tempted to let her linger for just a bit longer but when she moaned out his name, he intensified his effort. He felt her hands latch harder onto his head, her hips lifting even higher. He concentrated his licking to just the right spot.

"ALISTAIR!!!" she cried out.

He quickly sat up then flipped her over. He needed to take her, to claim her. He lifted her hips up and positioned himself behind her. He rammed his cock into her as he growled his desire. He pushed her head down to the mattress when she tried to get up.

"My female," he growled as he leaned over her. He could feel her body quiver with anticipation. He leaned over further, his mouth next to her ear. "Mine…" He licked her earlobe as he slowly thrust. He knew what she wanted, but he wanted to hear her say it. He licked her shoulder feeling her shudder. "Tell me you are mine," he said in his deepest voice. "Tell me female."

"You are my male," she said breathily. She tried to push her hips back wanting him to take her roughly.

He let his tongue circle her shoulder. "Louder," he growled

"You are my male!" she cried out.

He thrust his cock harder and faster as he bit her shoulder. He heard her cry out her orgasm. He kept her pinned under him, bit a little harder, growled a little louder, thrust harder and faster.

"Alistair you are my male…oohhh Alistair."

His orgasm hit him so strongly that he arched up and roared. He buried his cock to the hilt as his seed filled her. The intensity of his orgasm had been so great his body trembled as he collapsed down onto her. He felt her small body under him, he wanted nothing more to just lay like this, his large body protectively covering hers. But he knew his body weight would crush her. He allowed himself a few more seconds to lie like this until he heard her labored breathing. He rolled off of her.

"I love you, my female," he said as he tenderly stroked her back.

"I love you, my male." She smiled at him with such a look of contentment.

ဆာဆာဆာ

Alistair and Anne enjoyed the next two weeks together. They talked about either staying on Earth or going back to Malka. Alistair left it up to her, though she could see that he really wanted to go home. Adjusting to Earth was hard on him where as for her adjusting to life on Malka was pretty easy. She would get to be an animal doctor on Malka. She rather enjoyed her training with Tomar. And she had to admit Malka was beautiful. So what the heck was she thinking about. Going back to Malka would make Alistair happy and she had to admit it would make her happy too.

"Alistair I have decided I would like for us to go back to Malka," she announced over dinner.

"Are you sure?"

"Yes, very sure. But promise me that you will let me train with Tomar to become an animal healer."

"I promise. If being an animal healer makes you happy then that is what I would desire for you. Now I can drink the sacred juice so I can give you offspring."

"Nina mentioned something about that. So if you don't drink this juice I won't get pregnant."

"Yes. During the joining ceremony the male drinks the sacred juice. This is a Dascon tradition not a Larmat one. Since I was raised with Dascon people I chose to adopt their traditions."

"What makes you happy Alistair?"

"You, my female."

"Alistair…"

"Things will be different for you on Malka. You are my mate now so no other warrior would dare touch you. This even applies to the Larmat people. When their warriors offer a female protection she is much safer."

Both of them jumped to their feet when the front door burst opened and three very large Dascon warriors entered the house. Alistair reached back for his sword but it wasn't there. He had left it in the bedroom.

"Alistair we have been ordered to take you back to Malka to face Niro's anger. If you don't come willingly Niro has ordered us to kill you."

"What?!" Anne said, rushing to Alistair side. "Niro would have you killed?"

"If I don't go with them, yes they will kill me." He turned and looked at Anne. "I disobeyed his orders. I jeopardized the peace between the two clans. I must face my punishment, Anne."

"But I thought Niro was your friend."

"He is also the ruler of the Dascon people." Alistair looked over to the three males. "I will go with you peacefully. This female is my mate and I will not allow any of you to come near her. I ask that you give us a moment to gather our things."

"Be quick."

Alistair grabbed Anne's hand and led her up to the bedroom. He grabbed his sword and the book that contained his father's writings. "Take only what you need, Anne."

"Alistair, what will Niro do to you?"

"Whatever it is I will accept my punishment gracefully."

Anne was afraid. It felt like she was in a bad dream and couldn't wake up. She followed Alistair to the Rundal ship. It was the same one that took her to Malka. When they entered the ship she could hear the whimpers of a woman. The three Dascon warriors must have taken females. But she couldn't think about that now. All she could think about was what Niro was going to do to Alistair.

Chapter Sixteen

The trip seemed to last forever, but finally they had landed on Malka. Alistair was very quiet on the ride over to the main Dascon village. They were led to Niro's chamber by four warriors. The four stayed as Niro entered the chamber.

Alistair unstrapped his sword and let it fall to the ground, a clear sign that he wasn't going to resist.

"I ordered you to lead the Larmat people. What you have done could have jeopardized the peace I worked so hard to bring to the clans. Demos wasn't the warrior I wanted to lead the people and you should have known that he could have never ruled beside a Larmat warrior. But I knew you could. That is why I appointed you ruler."

"What has happened?"

"Thankfully nothing. Demos surprised me and allowed Mace to rule beside him. I suspect it was Nina who I should thank for this."

Alistair slowly walked over to Niro and came down to his knees. "I will accept any punishment I deserve. I am truly sorry Niro. But I needed to give my female what she needed most. Do with me as you will. Though I know I don't deserve it…promise me that you will look after my female."

"Alistair…" Anne tried to rush over to him but was stopped by one of the warriors. "Niro it was my fault he left."

"You should have stopped him from leaving."

"Leave my female out of this. Promise me Niro that you will take care of her."

"It is not my wish to kill you Alistair."

Anne breathed out a sigh of relief.

"However we are going back to the Larmat village and you will do what I ordered you to do. If you can't prove to me that you are capable of this task, you will leave me no choice but to banish you."

Alistair slowly came to his feet. He was relieved that Niro showed mercy, but at the same time he was ashamed.

"We leave immediately." Niro gestured to the warriors to take Alistair and Anne to the awaiting conjas.

It was a long two-day ride to the Larmat village. Anne had no idea just what Niro wanted Alistair to do to prove that he could rule the Larmat people.

When they entered the Larmat village a large crowd was gathering. Word must have gotten to them somehow. Alistair followed Niro up to where Demos and Mace were waiting.

"Demos I thank you for keeping the peace and I thank you Mace for helping him," Niro said. Both bowed their heads respectfully to him.

Niro turned to Alistair. "Prove to me that you can rule these people. Prove to me you can look beyond what you were born as and realize what these people need."

Nina grabbed Anne's hand as they watched Alistair go to the center of the platform.

Anne couldn't take her eyes off of him as he stood there so proud, so strong.

"People of the Larmat clan, I declare myself your leader," Alistair said in a loud, deep powerful voice. "I will kill anyone who breaks the peace that Niro wants between our clans. I will kill any warrior who dares challenge me. We are the people of Malka—it is time that we learn to live in peace."

"Who do you think you are half-breed that you should be our leader," a very large Larmat warrior yelled out.

Alistair pulled his sword out and lifted it above his head. "I am Alistair, the son of the grand Larmat warrior Tibor. His fierce blood runs proudly through my veins and I dare anyone to challenge my right to be the Larmat ruler."

Anne looked around when the Dascon warriors yelled out a battle cry, followed shortly by the Larmat warriors.

She looked at Alistair holding his sword high above his head. The pride she felt for him swelled inside her threatening to bring tears of joy to her eyes.

"Come my mate." Alistair turned and looked at her. She hurried to him and grabbed his hand. She stood beside him as he basked in the warmth of the Larmat people's acceptance.

Niro walked over to Alistair. "This is the warrior I wanted to lead the Larmat people to an era of peace." Niro smiled at him.

That look on Alistair's face was priceless to her. He had finally accepted who he was. She knew there would always be people who wouldn't accept him, but that didn't matter. She grabbed his hand tighter. She would be by his side no matter what. She knew between Niro and Alistair peace would be achieved in time.

THE END

.

"Protector of My Heart"

Robin Stevens never thought that her ordinary life would change in an instant. But when a large barbarian warrior from the planet Malka burst through her bedroom and carries her off to his world, her whole life changes forever.

Niro, the son of the Dascon clan leader Hakan, falls instantly in love with the little female that he was sent to collect. The females on his home planet are few in numbers due to a strange illness that wiped out half of them, still more were lost to the battles that continue to rage between the Dascon and Larmat clans. Though the earth women look as though they might be able to become mates for the strongest of Barbarian warriors, Hakan orders that only two would be taken, to make sure they could adjust to Malka.

Niro claims the right to be Robin's protector. Robin has no idea that by doing this Niro has proclaimed his love for her and his intentions of wanting to be her mate. The strong-willed Robin must learn to fit into the seemingly male dominated society of Malka. But together Robin and Niro find a love that will joined them forever. This is book one of Justus Roux's Barbarian's of Malka series

Justus Roux

"A Warrior's Will"

Nina Harris' life wasn't going so hot for her. Her love life stunk, her career if you could call it that was going nowhere. The only solace she had was her karate training. But after one of her karate classes, Nina gets abducted and taken to the planet of Malka. After spending the whole trip to Malka defending herself from a large barbarian warrior, Nina wanted nothing more than to speak to these barbarians leader and demand they return her to Earth.

Demos saw Nina walking off the Rundal ship in chains and Rai her would be protector covered in bruises. Never had he seen a female so brave, so able to defend herself before. He instantly is attracted to her. It is more than her beauty that captivates him, it is her spirit. He challenges Rai to become Nina's protector and wins. Her reluctance to accept him confuses but intrigues him.

Nina must adjust to the male dominated world of Malka without losing who she is. Demos both infuriates and excites her, and shows her an unconditional love she has never felt before. Will they be able to overcome the many obstacles that stand in the way of their happiness? Or are they to different?

This is book two of Justus Roux's Barbarians of Malka Series

www.justusroux.com

Website has excerpts of all Justus Roux's books, plus free stories by Justus and several talented guest writers. And a monthly contest to win Justus' books.

Printed in the United Kingdom
by Lightning Source UK Ltd.
113327UKS00001B/13